UNRELIABLE

A novel of suspense

Molleen Zwiker

Unreliable: A novel of suspense

Published by Scribe Publishing Company
Royal Oak, Michigan
www.scribe-publishing.com

Copyright © 2012 by Molleen Zwiker
Cover design by Jun Ares

ISBN 978-0-9859562-2-6

Library of Congress Control Number: 2012947445

Printed in the U.S.

DEDICATION

To my own "Amber," "Ashley," and "Jason,"
who have always had their mama's back.

NOTE FROM "AMBER": INSERT A

The first thing you need to know about my mom is that she's full of it. Honestly. You never know what she's going to say to whom, where, about what. The stories I could tell would boggle your mind. I'm not saying she's a pathological liar or anything as extreme as that, but she'd just as soon tell a stranger a tall tale than the truth, just for the hell of it. Embarrassed the hell out of us kids.

You want to know why we all moved away? I'll tell you. Although, now that I think about it, it's probably a different specific reason for each of us, but all with the same root: our mom. I guess I'm getting ahead of myself.

When my mom dropped out of Facebook and didn't answer my e-mails or phone messages, I freaked out. I mean, she makes me crazy most of the time, always has, but she is my mom. For all I knew, she'd dropped dead on her kitchen floor. It happens like that sometimes, you know. The healthiest, hardiest, just-passed-a-check-up-with-flying-colors person just checks out. Some odd undiagnosed disorder or another. For all I knew, I'd walk into her house and find her rotting corpse. Or a crime scene. Nice thing for a daughter to have to deal with.

My mom was chronically friendly to everyone, some stupid "entertaining angels unawares" thing. Wouldn't surprise me if someone she'd befriended offed her for the five remaining bottles of the six-pack of Miller Chill in her fridge. Things like that do happen, you know. See it all the time in the news and on those true-crime TV shows.

At least it wouldn't be for her money. My mom and money were like the flip sides of two magnets. Repelled each other.

But that's another story. For now, I just want you to know how all this came about. My mom went missing, and I drove up to Michigan from Georgia to find out why. What I found was several stacks of microcassettes on her kitchen table and a recorder. I can't even imagine why she bought something like that, but again, my mom always was unpredictable. I mean is. Is unpredictable. She wasn't lying in a smelly heap, and the house wasn't torn apart. There was no sign of violence or mayhem. No note, either. Her car was gone and she was gone and the house had that creepy stillness when no human has been there in awhile.

I knew better than to go question the neighbors. My mom was friendly, but only in a surface way. She'd impulsively haul in a neighbor's trash bin for them if they weren't home, but she'd never tell them her plans. She prides herself on being a good neighbor, but she doesn't 'neighbor,' as she called it. No coffee over the garden gate, no chit-chat at the mailbox. And she'd be majorly pissed at me if I contacted any of her friends.

There wasn't really anything else I could think to do but listen to the tapes. Obviously she meant me to, or for someone to. I mean, why else would she just leave them out like that? Besides, I wasn't in a hurry to turn around and go home.

UNRELIABLE

EARLY MIDDLE

It was an old family joke. We'd each said it hundreds of times. Whenever we were frustrated by bosses, co-workers, neighbors, inept drivers, significant others, we'd get to the end of our rant of the day and say, "God, I could've just killed her."

Or him, as the case may be. Then we'd pause, the perfectly-timed comedic pause, two beats, and the other would say, "But what would you do with the body?" And then we'd all laugh and the tension would dissipate, the frustration-causing event safely stuffed away, all anger deflated. This is what humor is supposed to do— defuse a tense situation. But what we sometimes forget is that at the core of every joke is a seed of truth. And that for a joke to work, someone has to be laughing.

This past July, the rubber band on my daughter's back snapped her to Michigan for her annual visit. "Mom," Amber said, meticulously planning her trip in advance. "Let's take a day and drive past all the houses we've lived in. I want to get some pictures for my photo journal."

"Sure," I said, stupidly, idiotically, unthinkingly. "That should be fun. We'll even stop for lunch at Tony's in Birch Run, like we did when you were little."

So simply. Just a mother and daughter on a photo-op down memory lane. How could I have been so careless? How could I have refused?

I know it sounds impossible, improbable, unlikely. But I just wasn't thinking. Somehow I'd managed to stuff my horrible memories so deep, had locked them so far down and away and out that I had functionally forgotten them. Or maybe not forgotten, but ignored them. What I did was so unlike me, so alien from who I was—or thought I was—that I somehow sifted it out of my mind.

I buried it, or flung it into a deep abyss, or into outer space like a metal cylinder of cremated remains sent into orbit. You can do that, you know, if you have enough money. If you have enough money, you can do anything you want—even after death. Or so I thought.

LATE MIDDLE

No doubt you've heard the saying, "You can't go home again." But of course, you can. It's just that "home" will have changed, grown smaller or shabbier with chipped paint or a mossy roof or someone else's kids' toys strewn about the yard. Sometimes the changes are for the better, say a new addition, perhaps a Mansard roof that doubles the previous square footage of living space. Or a new wraparound deck. Or you will have changed, grown more realistic, with a wider view of the world and different expectations, different perspectives. Different desires.

What we should really say is that, of course, we can go back to a house or apartment from our past; it just won't be home anymore. And we are powerless to change anything about any of it. So we need to be very, very careful about deciding to go home again, and we need especially to be prepared for what we might find if we do. We need to think very carefully about the past that crouches there, waiting to spring out at us to threaten our present, to devastate us with ugly truths we'd thought we'd buried along with the cocoa tin of Canadian pennies and plastic cowboys, a red tail feather from our uncle's African gray parrot, or a worn leather wallet. At least, that's the way it was for me, when I was foolish enough to go home again.

But let me start in the middle; I'll get to the beginning eventually. And then—the end.

I have three grown children, all of whom live in different states, far from me, so I don't get to see them very often. My sister—my half-sister, that is—once asked me what the hell I'd done to my kids to drive them so far away from me. I'd just laughed at her thinly-veiled attack on my mothering skills. Her two daughters, then in their early thirties, lived practically in her shirt pocket. Without saying it aloud, I'd had a similar thought about her: why had she so emotionally crippled her kids that they were afraid to leave her side, afraid to stake out lives of their own, independent and free? I had accomplished what I'd set out to do: give my kids wings.

I'd just never counted on how far from me those wings might take them.

My oldest, my only daughter, lives just south of Atlanta, Georgia. I specify Georgia because Michigan has an Atlanta, too, far north but still in the Lower Peninsula and nothing like Hotlanta, as they call it. When she was 21, my daughter visited a good friend who'd moved there, and she inadvertently fell in love. With the city, not the friend. It didn't take her long after coming home to decide to move, so she packed up her tiny blue '86 Geo Metro with what little it would hold and drove off without looking back. At the time, I thought that was cold of her. But she later told me she was afraid to look back, for fear of losing her resolve or breaking down in tears. God knows I had.

My second born, my first son, had similarly fallen in love with the climate of Florida and had likewise deserted the two-season state of his birth. We Michiganians like to say we have two, not four seasons: winter and the Fourth of July. That is a slight exaggeration, but not much. Like my oldest two, I prefer hot weather, hot and dry in fact, but unlike them I have never had the nerve to get out of the mitten. Wherever you travel, anywhere in the world, if you see someone holding up their left hand, palm out and pointing to the back of their hand, you can be assured they are from Michigan. Besides, Michigan does attach a rubber band to your back. You can leave, but you will just be snapped back when you least expect it.

My youngest, my second son, loves Michigan. In fact, his dream is to move even farther into the north, maybe even the UP, the upper peninsula, to find the coldest possible climate without having to leave the state. He laughs when I question his sanity. He wants to be a cop. All of this mess of mine could blow him right out of the water if he hadn't decided to change his last name to my maiden name. Legally, of course. Everything with him is by the book. So I hope his connection to me will remain hidden. It would be a shame to screw up his life again; he should retain the right to do that for himself. Ashley and Amber always had their own father's last name, and Amber has now added her husband's, with a hyphen, of course. So they, I sincerely pray, will also remain unaffected when all of this comes out. As it surely will do. No one gets away with murder twice.

MID-MIDDLE

On Amber's third day home, we began by driving past the two-story brick apartment complex on Woodbridge Avenue where her father and I had first lived. I pointed to the jalousie windows in the southwest corner of the second floor.

"J-Lousy, your dad called them," I told her.

"What were they thinking?" she said, shaking her head. "Jalousie windows were not invented for Michigan winters. Must've been fun."

"We could've chipped ice off 'em for drinks. If we'd been old enough to drink."

"Pull over, Mom. Let me get a picture."

And as she did, I noticed the greenish brass numerals at the front entrance: 2102. A 5, then; of course it would be a 5: Number 5s are temporary dwellings, suitable for single people, for people who are seldom home, not places to put down roots, not places to raise a family. I almost laughed out loud. How appropriate for our first

19

home together. My daughter's voice faded away as I remembered our brief residence in that apartment.

Scott and I were already in trouble when we visited that dreary dining room at the justice of the peace's house. Michigan has long since done away with the office of Justice of the Peace, but back then it was a no-frills way to get married, handy if a couple were "in trouble," the euphemism we used for knocked-up, preggers, in the family way. And we were that, too, or at least I was. Now that time has blown away the love-struck fantasy I lived in, I'm not sure that there ever was a "we" in our relationship. And what little might have been went down the tubes in a right hurry, let me tell you. So when I say we were in trouble, I mean yes, I was pregnant with what would become Amber, but our relationship as well. The pregnancy told the whole story.

Our six-month relationship had more downs than ups and was marked primarily by our breaking up, suddenly and painfully, then suddenly and painfully reconciling. Scott had given me a lovely milky opal ring, my birthstone, but it was in his pocket as often as on my finger. Like a ping-pong ring. At one of our breakups, he'd walked me to my car in his parent's driveway and asked for the damn thing back. Again. I slipped off the ring and threw it on the pavement and then ground it to powder with one furious stamp of my foot. It broke my heart to lose that ring, but at least he could never again ask for it back, only to re-offer it in a day or two. I might even have already been pregnant. I can't remember. Even after that, we got married.

My dad, whom I had most assuredly not told about

my condition, might have sensed something. The night before our wedding (I want to put quotation marks around the word because an ironic tone belongs there) I stayed up late making my own dress, an ivory brocade long-sleeved sheath. It was the second dress I had to make, as the first one, a white satin sheath with an A-line tulle overdress, ended up too small. I'd already gained ten pounds and the seams screamed.

As I hand-hemmed the dress, my dad pulled up a kitchen chair across from me. He had gone to bed once, but had gotten back up, so he sat in his blue and white checked pajamas covered by his white cotton terry bathrobe. He had poured himself a glass of milk and offered me one, but I declined. He watched me for a bit, the air between us heavy in unspoken concern.

Then, finally, after about a year and a half of screwing his courage to the sticking post, he cleared his throat and softly said, "You know, Honey, you don't have to do this."

And everything he meant was in what was not said.

I didn't look up, didn't meet his gaze, just kept stitching and stitching, watching my own fingers secure the fabric of my miserable future, and I even more softly replied, "Yes. Yes, I do."

And I did. Not just "have to" as in "have to get married," which was another silly euphemism of the time, but I truly felt I had to. What choice did I have? Of course I had to marry Scott. I had to do what was expected of me. I had no 'marketable skills,' as we call them now. I had only limited work experience: a few months at an ice cream parlor and a few more behind the lunch counter at S.S. Kresge's, a five and dime store which would later become K-Mart. Besides, I could not bear to stay in my father's house. I might have failed to be a daughter to be proud of, but I was determined to be a good mom. And good moms, at least in those days, were married.

So we stood side by side, I in my handmade dress, Scott in his borrowed blue suit which hung on him like a lame joke, and listened as the JP raced through the formalities. God knows what Scott was thinking or feeling—I never asked, wanting neither the truth nor a lie—but I was focused on the door behind the JP, willing my high school sweetheart to burst through and rescue me.

That sounds awful, I know, but it is the truth. Scott and I were so damned young and so damned stupid and so damned screwed up. We'd been so hot for each other and so clueless that being in heat is not, by a long shot, the same as being in love, or that being in love is not, by a long shot, the same as loving. That being parents is not the same as being ready to be parents. That being compatible in bed (or in our case, on couch) did not mean being suitable marriage partners.

Not that it mattered. The sexual compatibility, I mean.

"Mom?"

Amber's voice broke through. By the impatience in her tone, she'd said something I'd missed.

"Sorry, Honey. Just remembering. What?"

"I asked where was next. My list says Vermont Street. Is that right? How far?"

"Maybe ten minutes," I said, but I was still in remembering mode and slipped as easily into reverie as into gear.

"Do you want to talk about it?"

"No. Not really. We weren't here very long. A few months, I guess. All I could cook was spaghetti with canned sauce. And we had only a few pieces of hand-me-down furniture. It was pretty pathetic, really. We lived here when we found out your dad wouldn't be drafted because of his poor eyesight."

"That would've been Viet Nam? We were watching this documentary the other night and—"

And I went back to my memories.

From the moment we said "I do," he didn't any more. Want me, I mean. Just like that, like the flip of a switch. I'd expected the heat, the pleasure in each other's bodies to continue. But it abruptly stopped. We were over before we legally began but stuck it out for four years before tossing in the towel. By then we had Amber and Ashley. Their names probably tell the whole story. I'd spent most of my life with my nose stuck in books, so had a truly skewed view of life and love and marriage.

Scott had his own preferences in reading material, which I accidentally discovered one day when I got stuck in my father's mucky excuse for a driveway and we'd needed the jack. Hidden in the wheel well was Scott's library. I was so embarrassed—and so confused. Those books and magazines indicated in avid interest in the one thing he did not have any interest in with me. I left out that part when I toured the old home sites with

Amber. We've always been pretty open with each other, but I've tried hard not to run down her daddy in front of her, not wanting her to lose respect for him. As it turned out, he didn't need any help in that department, either.

"Good God, Mom, what a dump. Tell me it used to be nicer."

"Can't. It wasn't," I admitted, as we drove past the ratty little duplex on Vermont Street we'd moved into when we got kicked out of the first apartment for having a puppy. We'd smuggled her in and out in a laundry basket of towels, but got caught. We knew we weren't allowed pets, but I wanted her so badly. I was so damn lonely. I needed something to love and something to love me. She was a Norwegian elkhound-shepherd mix that we named Pepsi. My drink of choice. We got kicked out with little notice and less money. This little duplex was the only place we could afford that allowed Pepsi to stay.

As Amber asked questions and took pictures, I noticed the address: 901. Of course. Our apartment was a number one dwelling. The number of competitiveness, of having always to be on top, to beat out the competition. I keep my numerology to myself, mostly. I suspect my kids already think I'm off my nut. Maybe I am. But the address explains Scott's deal with the parking place. I pointed out to Amber the spot in front of the duplex where the oak tree had stood before it squished my car.

"I remember that story. But tell me again," she said, fiddling with her tape recorder. "For posterity."

There were only two parking places in front, parallel to the street, with more parking in back. Scott and the guy who lived on the other side of our apartment had a childish running battle about those two places. I'd wanted no part of the skirmish, being perfectly happy to park in back and waddle my huge pregnant self through the obstacle course of pond-sized potholes in the dirt driveway.

But one day the neighbor made the mistake of leaving his front parking space open and Scott leapt at the chance to one-up him. Scott nagged me into moving my car into it. For some reason this gave Scott a great deal of satisfaction, and he chuckled all evening, especially when our neighbor came home to find he had to park in back. He revved his engine and squealed his brakes and slammed his door—twice. Scott positively roared with laughter. As it happened, an especially strong windstorm came up suddenly in the night and toppled the ancient oak I'd parked beneath. If I'd refused to move my car, had refused to allow myself to be sucked into that infantile conflict, Scott's all-plastic Corvette would have been in the path of that tree. Now that, I thought, would have been funny.

A second memorable event happened in that funky little apartment: I fell in love with my huge belly. I'd felt my baby move many times. But one night as I lay soaking in the tub, my belly a gargantuan island high and dry out of the water, I felt her move and saw her at the same time. A small lump of knee or elbow moved slowly left to right. I saw her. My baby. My daughter. That was also my first natural high.

I'd heard the phrase, understood the concept, but now I felt it. Euphoria. She became real to me in that moment, no longer a theoretical baby. It was to get even better, but not in that apartment. The stench of the nearby pickle factory and the cramped quarters drove us to the rented house we moved to shortly before Amber was born. We drove there next, she loaded with her camera, I with my memories. Only some of which I shared.

Scott and I were so glad to get a little breathing room and two bedrooms that we scarcely noticed the rundown condition of the house on North Carolina Street. Again I noticed the numbers and mentally added the digits until there was only one left: 1607. So, doing the math: $1 + 6 = 7$; $7 + 7 = 14$; $1 + 4 = 5$. A 5 house. Of course.

If I had known back then that numbers give off vibrations that attract or repel specific energies, would I have still moved into the houses I did? In this case, probably. Renters can seldom be choosers. Remember, I said seldom. Sometimes they can. In our case, back then, the only numbers we were concerned with were the ones adding up to the monthly rent, which we could afford since Scott had caved to his father's pressure and taken a job at the shop.

So Scott, impeccably groomed and slightly effete Scott, became a shop rat. He came home smelling of machine oil and dripping with grime. The oil ate through his thick leather steel-toed shop boots at a rate of about a pair a month. He hated every moment of what would be a lifetime occupation, but at least he could afford to rent a house, and he could afford a wife and family. His resentment was palpable, but I was helpless to alleviate it. So I poured my energy into preparing for our baby and in trying to make the rented house a rented home.

"So I was born here?" Amber asked, although she perfectly well knew the answer.

"Well, this is where we lived when you were born. But you were born in Saginaw General."

Amber rolled her eyes, a teenage habit she never outgrew. "You know what I mean," she snapped as she pulled her camera out of its bag and rolled down the passenger side window.

"We sure could have used air conditioning back then. It was ungodly hot that summer."

"I suppose that was my fault, too," she said.

Here it comes again. Never far from the surface. Her resentment of me. Her assumption that I am criticizing. All I ever wanted was for us to enjoy each other's company. I've waited and waited all these years for the mother-daughter friendship to evolve. I've told myself that it was just a phase, that she would grow out of the tedious resentment of the mother. But it hasn't happened. Our time together is as fragile as—as what? I want the clichéd eggshells, but eggshells can be pretty damn tough. Have you ever noticed that? When you want to break them, sometimes it takes several good whacks and a thumbnail to get through. So I'm trying to think of something less clichéd and more accurate. Something that can be destroyed by the merest tentative stroke. I think of spider webs, or cob webs, but they, too, are deceptively strong. You have to work to break through them. Sometimes you have to get a broom. Snowflakes? Maybe as fragile as a snowflake. All you have to do to destroy a snowflake is breathe.

All I have to do to destroy a peaceful moment with my daughter is breathe. And some days, breathing is all I can think how to do.

As Amber snapped her photos, I noticed how empty the house looked. There were curtains in the windows and the grass was neatly trimmed, but the house seemed empty. Typical of a number 5 house. There is never enough energy to fill it up. Pour it in and pour it in as much as you like, the house will always seem empty. And not the emptiness of expectation, either. The emptiness of despair, a forlorn and cold emptiness. Even in a heat wave.

In that rented house, I began to explore self-expression through home decorating and took pride in the grass seed I sowed in the tiny bare front yard. The apartments offered no opportunity for those things.

More to myself than to her, I said, "It was so ungodly hot that we moved the bed into the dining room. With the front and back doors open, there was a cross-breeze that helped. Somewhat."

Amber said nothing, her lips squeezed into an angry thin line.

The bedroom windows had been painted shut, I remembered. So we couldn't open them. And we didn't have any dining room furniture anyway. So we moved the bed into the only place that made sense. Both sets of parents were appalled, damn near horrified, when they saw what we'd done. The shocking Bohemianism of it. I never understood their reaction. Still don't. It was simply practical. At least I could breathe. And we were as far from Bohemian as we could get. We'd screwed ourselves smack dab into the lap of convention: married, pregnant, employed, miserable. They should have been happy for us.

Amber knew all this, but I understood that she needed to hear it again, so I told her, as if it were by rote: "One night, ten days before you were due, we were watching television when I had a sudden craving for a beer. A beer, can you imagine? Ice cold. The craving was so overpowering that we called your dad's folks to ask them to buy us a six-pack. We weren't old enough to buy beer, just make babies."

"And they did?"

"Oh yes, driving the five or six miles to bring it to us. I drank the first half of the first can in one deep draught, then handed it off to Scott. I hated beer. Within an hour of this inexplicable event, my water broke. You were on your way."

I told her what a sweet baby she'd been and how I loved to cuddle her and how we'd have to jostle her awake when people came to see her because she was such a world-class sleeper. I told her how, at just a few weeks old, she'd scooch up to the head of her bassinet and sleep there with her bottom hunched high into the air. I told her how I knew, even then, that someday she would scooch herself right out of my life.

I told her about how mad her dad had gotten when the men putting on a new roof had come right into the house without knocking and scared me as I lay in bed nursing her. They thought the house was empty. When Scott complained to our landlord, I was confused. And delighted. I thought that meant he did care about me, about us. But then I realized it was just more king-of-the-hill posturing. More macho bullshit, like with the parking places.

Still, our stay on Carolina Street was as close to happy as we were fated to get, at least together. And I was happy to see, all those years later, that whoever lived there had also been inspired to put their own stamp on the house with pots of cheerful pink and white petunias and bright sassy marigolds on the porch and a brightly painted blue plaque for the house numbers.

When Amber was nearly one year old, we moved again, this time into a little yellow brick house that we bought for a song and a down payment "loaned" to us by his grandmother.

This house too, needed work, needed personalizing and updating, but it was outside the city and was ours. Amber and I drove out there next.

I hadn't been past this house for decades. Not that I'd been avoiding it, but my future moves were in other directions, and there was no reason to go down River Road. There, with Amber, I was surprised that the house was much as we'd left it when her dad and I divorced, including the black trim we'd painted the eaves. Again, our parents were askance, but we liked it. Others apparently had, too. The driveway was still unpaved, but a pole barn-type garage had been built at the end of it behind the house. The brick pillars still held the wooden slats for the fence, but the red barberry hedge I'd planted at the north edge of the property was gone. I couldn't see if the lilac I'd planted was still in the northwest corner. The house looked solid, stable, conventional and conservative. Which was appropriate, considering the address added up to 4. A nice, safe, predictable house. Perfect for solid, stable, conservative people. Which we were not.

"Tell me about the puppy and the toilet," Amber said.

She had no real memories of this house, but I'd supplied her with some of mine. Others I kept to myself.

"You were maybe two. It was summer and I was absorbed in something, laundry maybe, when I realized you were missing. I searched for you frantically, panic mounting, until —"

"I know, I know! You found me asleep with my head on the puppy."

"He'd curled up in the coolest place in the house: behind the toilet."

"Tell me about Dad and the drywall."

So I did. I'd been so impressed when Scott singlehandedly dry walled over the ugly knotty pine we both hated in the living room. And what a beautiful job he'd done on the floor-to-ceiling pantry he built in the laundry room, then the linen closet he built in the bathroom. I had no idea he could do any of those things. Neither did he. But he asked people and he read voraciously and he tried. And I thought the results were amazing. I told her about the day we bribed her into a little privacy with a bag of suckers. A rare moment of marital intimacy that undoubtedly gave us her brother.

"Sugar? Jesus, Mom, what were you thinking? No wonder I'm addicted."

Shit. Another land mine. Another of the thousands of trip wires to prove what a shitty mother I was to poor little old her.

I tuned her out as she ranted. How do I hate thee, Mother? Let me count the ways. If she but knew. At least she'd have more solid ground, fiercer weapons against me. But really, does the shit fall far from the bull?

Amber chastised as she shot her photos. As she did, I revisited the memory file called The River Road House.

It amazes me now that I, that we, tried so hard to appear to be a happily married couple. We could not have been further from it.

It wasn't that we fought as much it was we worked so hard to stifle our discontent. I had everything I'd thought to want for myself at the time—a home, a husband, a baby, and then another—but of course I had nothing at all. Inside, I was aching and hollow. The more I poured myself out for that home and family, the less I got back. Somehow I'd gotten the idea that if you just gave and gave and gave, then sooner or later, someone would give back. Scott was just plain miserable.

He didn't want me. He hated his job at the plant where his dad was a manager. He laughed at my suggestions that he take some college classes, that he explore his options. Maybe he didn't see he had options, that I would have supported any decision he made to find his own fulfillment. He laughed that I thought personal fulfillment was obtainable or even desirable. He laughed derisively and pushed me away if I dared make any romantic overtures toward him.

Then one day he requested that I wife-swap with a buddy of his from work and his buddy's wife. It was my turn to laugh, to make a smart-ass remark, something like, "Okay, sure, but I get Peggy." But his request hurt like hell. It was also the proverbial straw that broke my camel back.

He did not know, then or ever, as far as I know, that the high school sweetheart I'd unsuccessfully willed to rescue me from my wedding day had periodically popped by to see how I was. He'd never stepped foot into any of our homes, but had stood at the threshold with that sheepish grin that had so endeared him to me when I was fifteen and we first met. He always asked, "Are you all right? Are you happy?" And I always lied. Until he showed up shortly after the swapping request.

Can we stop here for a moment? I need to say something off the record. I need to clarify something. First, I know this is probably boring you. All this background. Just get to the killing, you probably think.

But it is important. I need for you to have the whole picture, to understand. To understand how all this mess happened. And I need to ask you please, please, please not to judge me too quickly. I know what I've done is inexcusable, unforgivable, but events in my life have shaped me as much as events in your life, events you could not control, have shaped you.

Yes, once we are adults we make our own choices, our own decisions, and we must accept the consequences for them. I'm not blaming anyone else or trying to excuse my actions. I ask only that you reserve judgment until the end of my story. I'm trying to be honest with you, trying to tell this as honestly as possible, but that will require me to say things you might not be comfortable hearing. This is not a defense of my actions, but a confession. A full confession. But I need it to be full by my definition. Please hear me out.

So there I was, more deeply heartbroken—and spirit-broken—than I would have imagined I could be. I felt utterly alone and utterly undesirable and utterly unloved and unlovable when—do I have to give you his name? Can I just call him "Hank"? He had nothing to do with what happened later. Thank you. When Hank dropped by—this time, I did not lie when he asked those same questions. How was I? Was I happy? We talked a long time, he standing outside the screen and I standing inside, our hands touching through the screen. I longed to fall into his arms, to let go, just once, just once let my anguish escape.

"Meet me," he said. "Come to my house. Be with me."

And I nodded: yes. Yes, yes, yes, yes, yes, yes, yes.

I lied to Scott and told him I was going to a Tupperware party at my step-mom's. My folks were a half-an-hour drive away and another back. Given two hours for the party and another for the imaginary helping her clean up, Hank and I had three-and-a-half hours together after I drove the fifteen minutes to and from the address he'd given me. Not that he'd needed to. I'd always known his whereabouts, as he'd known mine.

Scott reluctantly agreed to babysit, as if he were doing some huge unpleasant favor for someone, rather than spending time with his own children. That just fries me, you know? When some guy talks about "babysitting" his own damn kids. Does their mom "babysit"? Sorry, I got off track there for a second.

I went to Hank's, praying my stepmom wouldn't call while I was away. We spent very little time chatting on his couch. He showed me a picture of his beautiful wife who was in the hospital recuperating from having her gall bladder removed. He showed me the picture of their son, who was staying overnight with Hank's parents. Then he showed me his bed. We made love efficiently and quickly, too quickly for me to realize it was the first time for us in a bed instead of a backseat. We made love the way people do when they have very little time and a great deal of need. He wanted me. I needed him. And as he came, he called my name. He called my name. I was there with him, fully present in body and mind and soul. He knew who I was. I shivered with the thrill of being wanted.

Then we cried in each other's arms for all that we might have been but would never be to each other. We cried together for all the losses of each of our lives. And then I went home. I put my clothes back on in silence. Without a word, he held my face in his hands and kissed my tears.

I wiped away his tears with my palms, but they kept streaming down his face as fast as mine were. And I got in my husband's car and I drove home very slowly, thinking up story after story of why I'd been crying to explain away my red eyes.

But I didn't need to lie. Scott and the kids were fast asleep. I took a shower to wash away the fantasy of happy-ever-after and might-have-been and went to bed beside my cold, uncaring husband. And I've never for one second felt the slightest twinge of guilt or regret.

Hank and I never did that again. There was only that once, that one time that proved it wasn't me, that Scott's almost pathological rejection of me from the moment I became his wife was some problem of his. I was just the unlucky object of his lack of affection.

There's more to it, of course, all that "emotionally-absent father who set the tone for all the emotionally-absent lovers I'd litter my life with" theories, in which there may be some merit.

And of course, there is Scott's side of the story, which I can't tell you, because I have never known. It never occurred to me to ask or to expect a truthful answer if I had.

At any rate, my encounter with Hank had quite an unexpected effect on me. With my rigid ideas of right and wrong, one would expect me to crumble under the sheer weight of adulterous guilt.

But I didn't see it as adultery, probably because Scott and I were married in name only. There was no meeting of minds or hearts of spirits (to say nothing of bodies), no shared political or religious ideology, and damned little respect or affection or appreciation of any variety.

We'd been nothing more than the unsuspecting victims of the biological imperative: breed or die. Perpetuate the species. A hormonally-induced hit-and-run. What Hank gave me on that one illicit night was, paradoxically, self-esteem, confidence, and courage. Courage to face the inevitable: Scott's and my separation and divorce.

For the record, it was he who said the words first: "I want a divorce."

My immediate response: "You've got it."

Our little house was already on the market because we planned to build a new, larger house on a lot we'd purchased. By the time I realized I wanted to stay in the house after Scott moved out, we'd already accepted an offer. So the kids and I moved to an apartment. Amber and I doubled back to get pictures of the complex, which was much the worse for time and poor management.

"It didn't look like this back then," I answered the unasked question in Amber's eyes.

"Thank God," she said. "I remembered it nicer."

It had been—considerably.

I'd looked at less expensive apartments in less desirable neighborhoods but was not comfortable envisioning my kids playing with the street urchins among the rusted-out beaters perched on concrete blocks, littered yards and streets, two-foot-tall weeds. The complex was technically on Center Road, but tucked back from the busy township street. It seemed calm, quiet, and serene with its grassy hillock in the center courtyard, white brick buildings, and tidy carports which surrounded the complex like a protective moat. It was more money, yes, but I felt it was well worth it. Back then, at least, the grass was trim and green, but as Amber and I drove around, my heart sank.

Different management, clearly, or different owners or both. The buildings were unkempt, the grass gone to seed. Peeling paint and more litter. If it had looked like this when I first saw it, I would have chosen the el cheapo second story apartment in the city.

"Part of the can't-go-home-again syndrome, I guess," she said as I switched the conversation to the pleasant memories we shared: the three of us walking together hand-in-hand-in-hand to our once-weekly trip to McDonald's; the time she moved to her own 'apartment' by filling her pink plastic suitcase with dolls, books, and soda crackers and spreading a blanket on the landing outside our door and up five steps; trick-or-treating through the complex, she a bride with old sheer curtains as her veil and Ashley a toddling bumble bee in his yellow blanket sleepers that I'd striped with electrical tape; Amber starting kindergarten, skipping merrily off to her great school adventure as I sat sobbing and abandoned in my car.

But not all my memories of the three years we lived there were pleasant. She had grown up, was a woman already, not a little girl to be shielded from ugly truths, but I believe that a person's secrets belong to him or her, and my worst memory of the Center Road apartment was about Ashley, not Amber.

We hadn't lived there very long, maybe a month or six weeks, when Scott's sister Denise and her son moved into, not just the same complex, but the same building, the upstairs apartment on the other side of the stairs. I have never understood why she did that; it has always puzzled me, but I never asked. Denise and I were friendly toward each other, or maybe civil toward each other is more accurate. But we were never friends. When our paths happened to cross, several times a week, she always greeted me in that slow, drawn-out way that seeps sarcasm. And I would respond with a quick, cheery but insincere "Hi." I'd have been perfectly happy to ignore her altogether, but after all our kids were cousins and occasional playmates. So we tolerated each other for their sakes.

Now, I've never pretended to be anything like a saint in the sex department, but her choices, well, her choice, at least, was absolutely repulsive to me. Her 'boyfriend' was a much, much older man, a sleaze with that too-black-for-his-pasty-complexion hair (what there was of it) that screamed cheap dye job. He bore such a strong resemblance to her father that they could have been twins separated at birth and raised on opposite sides of the track. The boyfriend's side without running water, apparently, for he always looked like he needed a good hot shower and a lot, a very lot, of soap. God only knows what he did for a living; no one seemed to know, but he was at her place during times of the day when most people are busy earning a living. Not that I could talk, with my night job, but the point is that he was with her during the day when her son, Nathan, was also there. And I eventually had reason suspect that they were none too cautious about their activities in front of him.

Our little two-bedroom sanctuary was invaded the first time when one night as I slept, I was awakened by the sound of our door lock being thrown. I heard two men's voices coming from the darkened living room.

"Man, she's gonna freak," said the first.

"No shit," said the second.

"Hold on. This isn't her shit."

"Whadda ya mean?"

"Her shit. All this ain't her shit. Her stuff."

"Crap, man, we best split."

"No shit, man."

And then the click of the door and then the lock.

I'd been promised that the lock had been changed after the previous tenant moved out. Standard policy: the locks were always changed.

The second event involved Nathan and the son of the complex manager. Nathan had never been quite right. Slow and loose jointed. Denise was still spoon-feeding him in his high chair when he was three; she said it was less messy, but he clearly didn't have the coordination to do it by himself. His dad, her ex-husband, made his living by litigation. Not as a lawyer, but as a professional claimant. He'd laughed as he explained what he did when he 'went to work': strolling the malls or individual stores looking for 'opportunities.' At least once it was a clothing item slipped from its hanger (by him), that he'd 'tripped' on. Several times it was a vacuum cleaner cord across an aisle, and once it was a tier of glass display shelves he walked into, quite deliberately, scratching his own cheek.

By squeezing the slight scratch, he explained, he was able to make it bleed profusely. His favorite was the seams and edges of carpets which he'd discover slightly loose, then work more so with the toe of his shoe until he could, again, 'trip.' The beauty of it, he chortled, was that he almost never had to go through with the suit; most of the time the store's insurance company was more than happy to settle out of court.

And Denise chuckled along with him, amused at his unethical inventiveness, at least until they divorced. In setting the child support, the judge could go by only his earned wages, which were almost nil. The compensations stores and their insurance companies paid him were not considered income. I have no idea where he is now, but I can guess.

I don't remember the complex manager's son's first name, but I remember his last, and you would, too, if I told you. It was all over the papers at the time and became a local slang expression. In an infinitive verb form, 'to Fogelsongg' for years meant to drop something over an overpass onto the traffic below. That's what the kid's dad was in prison for. He'd dropped a concrete block from an interstate overpass onto a car, killing the driver and her unborn twins. Maybe there's a gene for mayhem.

At any rate, I was coming home from picking up the babysitter when I noticed the strewn clothing, furniture, and books in the courtyard in front of our apartment. At first, I did not recognize the items, but then I was close enough to see my grandfather's antique mantle clock, one of the few items I owned that I truly valued.

It was my own fault, I suppose. Because I was running late, I'd thought I could save the two minutes or so it took to let in the babysitter and the kids, and had left the door unlocked. One time, just that one time. How could those two six-year olds have known they had that one and only one opportunity to vandalize our place? An instinct for criminal opportunity? We had so little to begin with, even less of it of any value, but there it was. I knew who'd done it; that is, I knew it was Nathan. The other kid's complicity was a surprise; I barely knew him. I did the only thing I could think to do: I called the police. I refused to press charges, but asked the officer to scare the hell out of the kids by talking to them very seriously, as if they were adults.

Oddly, the other kid's mom, the complex manager, came to face me and to offer to help retrieving our things. My former sister-in-law, my kid's Aunt Denise, did not. But a month or so later, she came to my work place, to let me know that she'd forgiven me.

"For what?" was my question.

"For calling the cops on my Nathan," she said, sort of self-righteously. "I've decided to forgive you."

And then, God help me, I began to laugh and could not stop. In that moment, I could see the poor kid's future as if it were a done deal. And I was right. The last I heard, Nathan was in prison—again.

Hypocritical of me, I suppose. Considering.

After the trashing, I began to look for another place. Has that ever happened to you? Have you ever found that what seemed like safety was danger? I've never quite found that safe haven I've sought all my life. Now I know 'safe haven' to be an oxymoron, right down there with 'financial security' and 'job security' and 'happily married.' But back then, I was still naive enough to keep searching.

Money was hard to come by, but when I calculated how much I'd paid in rent in the time we lived in the apartment, I almost threw up. I began to consider home ownership. My house obsession began in earnest as I looked at—and rejected—one place after another. Too run down. Too flimsy. Too far out of town. Too nice (code for too expensive). Too conventional. Too little yard. Too much yard (too much lawn mowing). Or it simply didn't 'feel right.' I couldn't have explained it better back then, but now that I know a little about numerology, I could.

In numerology, for example, I would never be drawn to an 8 house.

I would be more attracted to a 3 house (which fosters creativity), or, when the kids were still home, a 6 house (which is a great place to raise them or for a day care). The apartment complex was a 2 after we factor in the apartment letter and number. Number 2 homes are generally unlucky, being fraught with conflicting natures, an inherent duality. The apartment was not the last of the unlucky places I've lived, and did not bring the worst luck. Worst was yet to come.

During the last few months we lived in the complex, Amber came to me one day. She was clearly upset, but reticent about telling me what was bothering her, which was uncharacteristic of her. My daughter has always been upfront with people, telling them exactly what she means. She was only six, but sometimes seemed much older, much wiser.

"Mommy," she faltered. "I think I have to tell you something."

"Okay," I said.

"Well, I think it may be a bad thing."

"That's okay, Honey. You can tell me anything you need to. Any time," I'd said, or words to that effect.

"It's about Ashley, Mom."

"Okay, Baby, I'm listening."

"Nathan did something to him."

"Nathan?" I asked, trying to quell my rising panic. I'd gone cold inside, and Amber seemed to recede, to grow smaller and farther away, as if I were looking at her from the wrong end of binoculars. "What did Nathan do?"

But I suddenly really and truly didn't want to know. I could not breathe as Amber screwed up her courage and resolve.

Finally, she said, "Nathan put Ashley's pee-pee in his mouth and sucked on it. He told me not to tell. He said he'd beat me up if I told."

And the cold shell that had formed around me turned to fire. I had to struggle not to let my fury show in my voice. I didn't want Amber to think I was mad at her, that she'd made a mistake in telling me.

I choked on my next words as I struggled to remain in control of my raging emotions. "He's not going to beat you up, Baby. You did the right thing by telling me.

Thank you. Let's make sure Nathan never gets another chance to be alone with Ashley, okay?"

"Okay," my little girl said as she buried her head in my chest. I was afraid that if I ever laid eyes on that little creep again, I'd wring his neck. It would be so easy to trip him on the stairs, to crack his horrid skull on the concrete. To mix him up a nice little anti-freeze Popsicle. I stepped up my search for a house, far from that little cocksucker Nathan.

Finding a house is like finding a husband: pretty easy if you set your standards low enough. I bought the next house I saw.

My first house was tiny and on a tiny lot right on a state road. And it felt right. Now I know why: it was a 3. I have always been happiest in 3 houses. Best of all, it was mine. No horny neighbors above my head, no drunks across the hall, and best of all: no Nathan.

My great-aunt decided that the best time to give me my modest inheritance was when she was still alive and could see the benefit it would bring. A wise and generous woman, she gave me the down payment.

Amber and I headed there next, a good half-hour out of town. Into the country.

"You were already pregnant with Jason by then?" she asked.

"Yup. And his donor was still in the picture. For a little while, anyway."

"Did you love him?"

"I don't know. I liked him. I liked a lot of things about him. He was tall and smart and funny and creative and had these amazing blue eyes. A startling blue.

Almost hypnotic."

"What happened, Mom? Why'd you dump him?"

"I didn't. He dumped me."

"Why?"

"Damnedest reason."

"He found out you were pregnant?"

"Nope. He knew that. And accepted it. Willingly. I think he liked the idea of a family, of you kids and the one I was carrying."

"Jase?"

"Yup. He was so solicitous of me when he found out. He helped us move into the little house on Albee and wouldn't let me carry any of the heavy stuff. Cute, you know? But I'd carried two babies before and knew that pregnant ain't sick and it ain't weak. You can't shake a baby loose that easy. If you could, there wouldn't be such a thing as abortion."

And then I gasped at my absolute stupidity. Just like me to be blabbing away and not anticipating the land mine. So there it was, floating still in the air between us: the A word. I steeled myself for another explosion from my daughter, although I could not guess what form it would take. Would she accuse me of throwing it in her face? Would she melt down in a sobbing pool of regret and remorse? Would she accuse me of guilt-tripping her?

That had been her favorite, when in her teens I would try to get her to understand that actions have reactions, that every behavior has consequences that affect more people than simply the doer. If there is such a word. Doer? Do-er? That guilt is a good, healthy, normal reaction to bad behavior. And that guilt isn't even what I wanted her to feel. I wanted her to acknowledge responsibility for her actions. All of which, now, seems so horribly hypocritical of me.

But there was only a momentary pause between us as I drove the last few miles to the little house.

"Then what? Why'd he dump you?" Amber asked.

"Well, he found out it was his."

"And?"

"Couldn't accept it."

"I'm confused. Couldn't accept what? Did he love you?"

"He said he did. Once. I blew the standard, expected response, and he never said it again. He'd dated a friend of mine—that's how we met—and she knew it was his and told him. But he said he and his first wife never used protection and neither had he and any of the other women he'd been with, and none of them ever got pregnant. So it couldn't be his."

"Fuzzy logic. And that was the end of it?"

"Pretty much. He did come out to the house one more time. God knows what for. But a buddy of mine was over—a guy—and when I opened the door, Jase's donor took one look at him and turned around and left. I've never seen him again. I know where he lives; he's in the phone book. But you know, my flags were already up because of the eclipse."

"Eclipse?"

"Yup. When we were seeing each other—I was already pregnant by this beautiful, educated, funny, kind man—"

"Oh yeah, a real prince, Mom."

"There was a lunar eclipse. It was all over the news that day, so when I was at his apartment that night, I kept checking out the window to see if I could see anything. And I could. It was so clear. I kept asking him to come see it, too, to share it with me. But he refused. Over and over. He didn't believe me. He didn't believe there was an eclipse. It was really weird. The next day, he called to apologize, to tell me that everyone at work was talking about the eclipse and asking if he'd seen it. Then he realized I hadn't been pranking him. Real weird. I'd never pranked him, or anyone for that matter. I thought pranks were childish and kinda mean at the core, you know? Something nasty about humiliating someone else, even in fun. If you can call that fun."

"And?"

"And so how would he ever believe my baby was his? And what would life be like with someone who didn't believe a word I said? Who would not or could not—believe me? Who thought I was, at best, pranking him, but at worst, lying?"

"Could Jase be someone else's? Could you have been wrong? Was there anyone else?" Amber has always had a gift for asking the one question you wish she wouldn't.

Ouch. There it was. My opportunity to withhold an ugly truth from my daughter, my now-grown married woman daughter with whom I'd tried always to be honest. As honest as possible, that is. But no. Said's said, and done's done, as my grandma used to say.

So I had no real choice.

"There was someone else just before we met. That

same buddy, actually, but he had a 17 year-old daughter and a 16 year-old vasectomy scar. It was only a couple of times. There wasn't any real passion between us, and he wasn't very good at it. Alkies never are. Plus, he was unreliable. Once I met Killer Blue, the other guy and I slipped into an easy friendship. Besides, he was short, slight, and dark, with brown eyes."

"Not like Jase."

"Nope. He looks just like his donor. Tall, smart, funny, creative. Those same stunning eyes. A slight duck walk."

"And paranoid as hell."

"Ya, well, it never occurred to me that paranoia was an inheritable trait."

By this time, we were at the tiny house I'd bought back then. On the day we moved in, I'd planted a Russian olive tree not much bigger than a stick. It was Jason's tree, and I got a nasty start to see it had been cut down. It had grown so tall so fast with its silvery gray-green leaves. A shiver of apprehension passed through me. I wanted to turn around, not to finish our tour of my past. Our past. I should have, of course. I see that now. But then, on that day with Amber, I kept going. With a quick heartfelt prayer that my son would not similarly be cut down, we pulled over onto the shoulder to get our pictures. The willow tree on the other side of the driveway from the house had been hacked brutally, and we could see why: the present owners were starting a serious remodel. We'd considered that—Tim and I.

"So that's when Tim entered the picture?"

Amber startled me with her question so close to my

thoughts. Many people have told us over the years how much alike we are. This has flattered me, as she is so much more than I ever could have been, so much more talented, more successful, prettier and smarter. But for her these remarks have been insulting. I have been so much less than she would ever want to sink to. Our resemblance, such as it is, is not in appearance so much as in gestures, in wit and humor, in temperament. For better or worse, I am her mother. And blood tells. Always has, always will. Now I wonder what she would think, will think, when the truth comes to light. It kills me to imagine what she will think. Feel. Do. For even if no one ever links her to me, she will know. She will always know what kind of person her mother really was.

"Tell me about him," Amber prompted.

"You remember him."

"Tell me how you got hooked up with him in the first place."

"I've told you all this," I said.

"I know."

"A dozen times."

"I know."

"So?"

"So tell me again, Mom. It fits the day."

So there I was, a single mom of two-and-a-third kids. My income was still limited, but my house payment was considerably less than rent. It was quiet out there, and we lived closer to my folks, who loved taking the kids on weekends so I could pull long shifts at work.

Telling them I was pregnant wasn't too much fun. They first suggested an abortion, which was out of the question for me. After all, I was 25, not 15. Obviously, I wanted this child. He was not an accident. Then they suggested I adopt out my baby which I replied to by saying it was a great idea and while I was at it, I might as well adopt out the first two, too. They never said another word about adoption.

I had a nice car, nice looking, dependable, and economical. I had a house of my own with no oversexed overhead neighbors and no ex-sister-in-law and no Future Felon of America nephew. I had a constant breeze.

And rats.

"Rats? Mom? Yuck. I don't remember that part," Amber said.

"Well, it's not like I pointed them out to you. I didn't want you kids to see them," I said.

Heavy rains had flooded the deep ditches behind the house. And with the debris ditches seem so diligently to acquire, the torrent also washed my way a plague of field rats. As I complained about them one night at work, one of our regulars offered to come out to help set the poison traps. He'd briefly dated one of my co-workers, so I was able to check his credentials. She assured me he was harmless enough, as lacking in personality as looks, the kind of guy you don't notice until closing time and then only because he is the only one still around. And still willing. Or able.

My pregnancy was no secret, but seemed unimportant to Timothy Michael Whittacre. He never asked any questions, and I never offered any secrets. He showed up as promised, brought the poison, which he paid for, and refused reimbursement. He set the bait, explaining how it worked: the rats were attracted to it as a food source. Actually, he said, it was more like dessert to them. Like candy. Even if they weren't hungry, they'd gobble it up. And that what the poison did first was make them horribly thirsty, so they would seek water. Tim said it was very important that we put out pans of water for them, as if they were treasured pets, because the water activated the poison which, in effect, ate them up from the inside out. Tim said that rats lacked the ability to regurgitate, so when the poison started eating up their innards, they couldn't get rid of it by throwing up, as we do when we eat something bad. Or like dogs and cats and most other mammals.

He came back a few days later to clear the yard of dead rats. Then he noticed the back door window was cracked and offered to replace it. When he came out a few more days later, he brought a sheet of acrylic instead of glass. For the kids, he said, so it would be safer for them. He also brought pizza and pop for me and the kids, for all of us together. It reminded me of a dog I once had, a runt of a black lab, who came into heat. Our first clue was the many neighborhood male dogs vying for her attention on the back porch. One of them brought her half a woodchuck as a bed present. We got her fixed.

Each time Tim came out, he found another reason to return, and each time he'd up the ante. He'd stay longer and longer and be gone less and less. He told me pretty much what my co-worker had about his past: he was divorced; his wife and daughter lived in Midland, one of the tri-cities I'd just moved us out of. Because the stories matched, I didn't question further. A person has a right to some personal privacy, I believed. A right to keep a few details to himself. Or herself. Much later, I'd find out the truth, but by then it didn't matter. Not one dead-ass iota.

I'm not sure at exactly what point he actually moved in with us or at what point I realized he had. He was a very taciturn man. Taciturn is another word for secretive. He had many secrets. But he was easy to have around because he was so damned reliable and made so few demands. TV, a few hot meals, some sex now and then.

"Most of my memories of this house are good ones," Amber said. "The bike I got for my birthday and racing Tim on the back road."

"Yeah, right, until you hit the pothole and wiped out. Chipped your front tooth. God, I was mad at him."

"But I told you it wasn't his fault, Mom. We were having fun."

"What kind of grown man needs to compete with a little kid?"

"Mom, we were just having fun."

"I know. I just—I've always hated seeing you kids get hurt. You'd understand if you—" Somehow I stopped myself, but not in time.

"Mom. WE. ARE. NOT. GOING. TO. HAVE. THIS. DISCUSSION. AGAIN. Don't go there."

But of course, the problem is that we've never gone there. We've never had this discussion in the first place.

After it was over, she told me what she'd done and why she did it. Period. I've never told her how her decision affected me or how it hurt that she made it without asking my advice. But I suppose she knew what I would say, and didn't want to hear it. It was an accident; she took care of it. Period. End of story. Except it hasn't worked that way. It is not in the past, ever; it sits between us always, shapes our conversations, defines our relationship. Or lack of one. She has never wanted to hear my anger, but it is pain I felt. Sorrow. I raised her to make her own decisions, to not need me. And now she doesn't. So I succeeded. Damn me.

"I remember the school bus, too," she says, skillfully (or unconsciously) steering us away from the unspoken. "I remember how excited I was to be taking the bus. A school bus!"

She says it in the exact voice of her seven-year old self, all innocent awe and anticipation. "I was so excited I was out by the road half an hour early. Then the bus just sped right by. That broke my heart."

"I know, Honey. The driver hadn't gotten the word that there was a new stop on her route. It got straightened out right away."

"I know, but it was the first day. I never forgot that disappointment."

"And you used to practice your tap steps while you waited for the bus each morning."

"You knew?"

"Yup. I used to watch you."

"You watched?"

"Yup. Kept my eye on you until you were safely

inside the bus."

"I didn't know that, Mom."

"I know. I didn't want you to know. I wanted you to feel capable, independent. I didn't want you to think I didn't trust you."

"Did you? Trust me, I mean?"

"Of course, Honey. It's the rest of the world that scared me shitless."

"Hey, you know what else I remember? I remember Ashley painting his name in foot-high letters on the side of the house, then trying to blame me."

"But I knew you hadn't done it. Kids don't write other kid's names on things; they write their own. Besides, you knew how to write his name. He misspelled it the way he always did, transposing the 's' and the 'h'."

Amber shook her head, smiling and rolling her eyes.

"I don't remember what happened next. Did you spank him?"

"Nope. I made him clean off the writing with scouring powder."

"What about the piano?"

"What about it?"

"I just remembered the piano."

"Yup. An old upright I always meant to refinish. I hated the old, almost-black varnish."

"What happened to it?"

"What do you mean?"

"I don't remember it in the Lincoln Road house."

I paused, wracking my brain. I didn't remember it there, either. I could see it against the north wall of the apartment, and against the north wall of the living room in the little house. But nowhere in the next house. Did we leave it behind? Why would I leave a piano behind? The piano was simply missing from the file.

"I don't remember, Honey. I just don't know."

"Maybe Tim didn't want to move it, Mom. It weighed half a ton, I bet."

But that didn't fit either. Between my dad and Tim, they could have moved it. My dad and I had moved it in, after all. I'd gotten it free for the hauling away, and Amber needed a practice piano. What happened to that freaking piano?

"Never mind, Mom. It isn't important. Mom? Mom? Let it go," Amber was saying. But I barely heard her, couldn't break my focus on the missing piano. I kept seeing it there. On the north wall of the living room. Right next to the door to the bedroom.

"Oh, my God, Mom," my daughter interjected, her hand on my arm, "Do you remember Tim's appetite?"

Tim was tall and thin with an incredible appetite. His favorite pastime was hunting for all-you-can-eat dinner buffets, where he would shut down the steam table. Eventually, I refused to go to dinner with him in those sorts of restaurants. It might have been entertaining if I hadn't found it so revolting. To keep eating and eating and eating long after his hunger was sated seemed indecent. Vulgar. Obscene. The satisfaction it gave him to horrify waitresses and managers seemed nearly sadistic. And the worst of it was that he never gained an ounce. In fact, he seemed to get skinnier and skinnier by the month. Naked, he reminded me of a Flatsy doll, like Gumby if you know who he was, because sideways he would almost disappear. Unless he had an erection.

It was his naked scrawny body that one day began a flood of repressed memories I'd spent my whole life squashing down into the deep, dark hole where they belonged.

Late one afternoon early in our relationship, we had sex for the first time. My folks had my kids for the day, taking them somewhere fun, Deer Park maybe. Mom and Dad didn't much like Tim or didn't much like his living with us without the sanction of holy matrimony. I got the impression that they thought if they gave us enough time alone, I'd get tired of him faster. Or that I'd get him to marry me. So we were alone. I was already lying in bed, watching him undress, intrigued by the flatness of his body in profile.

Suddenly he said, "Time to take a little nappy."

And something happened to me. Have you ever seen those shots in movies where a character is standing still in the foreground and the background is receding fast? I can't explain it any better than that. I felt as if I were lying perfectly still in the bed, but the present was retreating fastfastfast behind me. Time—some 23 years—did not melt away so much as it swished away, too fast to recognize even the tiniest detail. I felt empty. And frozen. There was no desire in me. No happiness or joy or fear or curiosity or anything. Only acceptance. What was about to happen had happened before, and I was as powerless to resist in the present as I had been in the past.

I'd been left with this man, a tall flat skinny man. Again. Where was my mommy? Where was my daddy? It was time for a little nappy. We'd played the heels-over-head-as-the-dog-went-to Dover game and now it was time for a little nappy.

Tim lay down beside me and I automatically rolled away from him, onto my side. I knew how to take a little nappy. I was a good girl and did what I was told. I was a good girl. This man would play with me, bend me forward to do somersaults, over and over. Head over heels as the dog went to Dover. Oopsie Daisy. In my dress. He put his hand on my bottom to help me go over. Over and over. Then it was time for a little nappy. Tim put his penis between my legs, not inside me, but against my labia, and rocked himself to sleep. Just like the flat man did. And he held me tight so I could not get out of the bed. And I remembered. Something inside of me died that day, and something else was born.

I told Amber none of this.

My dad always answers my questions about my past as if they were about his past and I have no business asking anything at all. He has never seen that it is my own past I want to own. Ugly or not, I want to know. I have a right to know. A need to know.

But when I ask, whatever I ask, all I get is, "I don't know, Honey. I don't remember." Sometimes this is accompanied by, "It was such a long time ago."

He sees memory as a river that carries away everything that enters it, sweeps it all away into the deep blue ocean so it can never be isolated, identified, reclaimed. Perhaps, for him, this is true.

But for me, memory is an unimaginably huge filing system, perhaps a whole warehouse of filing cabinets. Some of the files in some of the drawers are easy to access, up front, eye level, clearly labeled. Others are stuffed in the farthest drawer of the farthest cabinet. Dusty and unmarked and forgotten, perhaps deliberately. Maybe even chained and locked with the key long gone, dropped off a train bridge, maybe. But still, the file is there. Everything is there. We just have to know where to look. Or for how long. Or in what light. And sometimes the file will just appear, who knows why, on our desktop. There it all is, spread before us, all the facts and figures and statistics. Perhaps photos. No. Always photos. In color, 8x10 glossies. Outlines in chalk.

For example, say I want to know, am trying to remember the address of the big red brick house on Gratiot Road we lived in when I was in the seventh grade. The second half of the seventh grade. That house is not even there anymore. Where it used to be is now a diagnostic imaging center, with center spelled affectedly 'centre.' So I can't drive by and take a picture of the place we lived in. Where my grandpa taught me to make rhubarb sauce from the rhubarb that grew at the side of the barn behind the house. Where I made a pathetic yarn doll lapel pin so I would not be forgotten by our live-in babysitter whose parents demanded she move right back out again because they did not approve of her being a live-in babysitter for a single dad's three kids. Where I had my first period and where my dad stopped hugging me because I started to wear bras.

But I can go digging through the dusty old file drawers until I find the picture of the dark red brick four-square with its white trim and expansive front porch. And I can then pull back and back from that picture until I can see the rusting metal rural mailbox at the side of the road just left of the driveway with the house numbers painted on it in flaking black paint— 1300! See? If we want to, if we are determined, if we try—really try, we can access any information we want or need.

So, to me, "I can't remember" is code for "I don't want to remember" or "I have no need for that memory" or "It is none of your business." None of your damned business, in fact.

So my birth mother's parents' names are lost to me, as are the names of all of her brothers and sisters. Somehow, to him, these facts—which might help me find more information about that branch of my heritage, my gene pool, is not any of my business. It belongs, somehow, to him. Or to the oblivion of the open sea.

Of course, there may be another meaning for the code phrase "I don't remember." It could also mean "I truly do not know; I have never known; I have never even cared to know, to be bothered with information that does not directly affect me." Maybe.

All of which, as I've said, I kept to myself. I have never told Amber, or any of the kids for that matter, much about my childhood. The basic facts, sure, but no details. Amber knows that the mother I refer to as my birth mother (a phrase adoptees use) split when I was five or so, after the state of Texas took us away from her and placed us in an orphanage. She knows that my father eventually gained custody of us and raised us on his own, except for an ill-fated 18-month marriage to my first stepmother, a nutjob my brothers and I unaffectionately called At Falice. Behind her extremely broad back, of course. Amber knows that her grandfather married Janice a week before her father and my marriage, such as it was. Janice is the only grandmother she and the boys have ever known, the only one they will ever know. She knows that Janice, who had no children with her first husband or with my father, loves her and the boys as fiercely and devotedly as any grandmother ever could. And that is enough.

I know what you are thinking. Sheherazade, the alleged storyteller of the Arabian Nights. If I can keep spinning tales, if I can keep you distracted, I can save myself. And my family. But that isn't why I'm bringing up all these seemingly unrelated stories. Mostly, it is so you can understand, can comprehend the incomprehensible. So you can judge me fairly. I'm allowed that, am I not? But I just realized that there is another way all this is functioning, a surprising way. Through putting all these disparate parts together for the first time, lining them like this in chronological order, I am beginning to see a pattern in these events and in my response to them. Perhaps I am more like my father than I'd thought. Perhaps I've chosen not to see the pattern before so I wouldn't have to face up to the logical consequences of my own actions.

My father always had a fantastic memory for dramatic lines, for poetry. Many times throughout the years he has quoted from William Henley's "Invictus": "I am the master of my fate / I am the captain of my soul," being his favorite lines. This is a poem, I might add, that I've long hated. The sheer arrogance of the speaker. Who is the master of his own fate? None of us. We may be the master of a given moment, or of our next action or choice. But fate? If we are the masters of our own fates, there is no such thing as fate. It is an oxymoronic claim. By definition, fate cannot be mastered. That's what I've always thought. Until now.

I am one house away from telling the story that we are here for. And when I'm done, when all the facts as I know them are on the table, it is not the state, nor society, not a jury of my peers who will decide my fate. I will decide. I have already decided. My plans are almost complete, meticulously stitched together, right sides facing, corners squared exactly so.

My life is functionally over, anyway. I've cut off all my connections, refusing to speak to anyone I love for fear I'd blurt out my intentions or that by some inadvertent slip of the tongue or tone of voice, I'd tip them off. Or flat-out confess. I've discontinued phone service, which includes the internet. I began this severance shortly after Amber and my photo journal journey, when the memories all came back and the new threat presented itself, and I realized the risk of speaking to anyone. The urge to confess is as overpowering as the urge to disclose my newest plan. So I truly have no choice. I'm sure you'll understand—eventually. But before I secure the future, I must disclose the past. So we need to return to the middle.

Tim worked at the biggest manufacturing plant in town and had since he'd turned 18. So he made decent money, and when my employability ran out at the end of my eighth month, he didn't seem to mind picking up my slack. And then he was supporting us entirely, except for the pittance of child support I received from Scott. I half-heartedly mentioned going back to work a month or so after Jason was born, but Tim said he made enough for all of us, that I could stay home as long as I wanted to. And I wanted to. I loved taking care of my family full-time. I had the sweet luxury of time to pamper my family with homebaked breads and slow-cooked meals and to dabble in some arts and crafts. I learned to macramé and the second quilt I ever made won a blue ribbon in the county fair. I reveled in experimentation with other needle arts (although I never mastered tatting) and with home decorating. I made the fatal mistake of relaxing.

The little house had something like 800 square feet of living space. Within a year of Jason's birth, we were looking at alternatives to ease our cramped home. We considered building an addition but couldn't decide on a floor plan we both liked. There was plenty of room in the front of the lot, but every plan we came up with seemed awkward, with no flow. It did not occur to us to build up, just out. As we wrestled with alternatives, two things happened: my parents increased their pressure on me to marry Tim, and the house next door to them went on the market. At half-again the square footage and many times the yard, it seemed a viable choice. Besides, since that other house needed so much work, it was listed at a price that was beyond reasonable. So I made an offer, then listed my little shoebox of a house, making an appreciable return on my investment. I'd made my first profit on real estate, but not my last. The deal on the new old house (a land contract so the owners could have monthly payments and collect the interest themselves) had to be done in my name only. Tim had reluctantly confessed that he was not really divorced yet. He and his wife, he told me, were still legally married and she was dragging her feet on the divorce, hoping, no doubt, he'd change his mind and return. This was fine with me. I liked owning my own home; I liked having things in my own name.

And I had a ready excuse not to marry him. Bigamy is not part of our family tradition. Other facts about Tim had slowly surfaced. At the time, I thought he simply needed to feel safe with me before he could divulge the more painful events in his past. He told me they'd had one child together, a son, who had died in infancy. SIDS, he told me. Sudden Infant Death Syndrome. Couples rarely survive the death of a child. Have you noticed that? Guilt, maybe, or blame. I was angry at first that he'd lied to me about having a child. But he explained, his face taut with pain, that it was easier for him to pretend the boy was still alive than to admit the truth—even to himself. I should have questioned him more deeply. I realize that now, but at the time, I slipped easily into an empathetic state of imagining how devastated I'd be if anything had happened to one of my own babies. So I let him off the hook.

Amber and I slowly drove to the next house, the last one of the day, as it would turn out, and I dreaded it. I steeled myself as we drove the four miles and ached to turn around, to skip it. But how to explain a refusal? A sudden headache? A pain in my stomach or back? I never acquired the useful skill of vomiting at will. Besides, Amber and her brothers had spent so much of their childhood at my parent's house that she thought of it as a second home and wanted a picture of it, too.

The house on Lincoln Road was a story-and-a-half cinder block square. It had never been painted as many cinder block houses are, so it was a drab gray. If I owned it now, I'd power-wash it. Or sand blast it. One dormer in the attic bedroom overlooked the worst imaginable excuse for a front porch, with rotting wood and a sagging roof and floor. We joked about strong winds doing the demo for us.

Here's another cliché that is actually quite an accurate description: my blood ran cold. Mine did. By the time we'd driven that short distance between houses, I was thoroughly chilled. I'm not sure what I expected that day with my daughter, what I expected to see or hear or feel. Given what I knew was planted there, I guess I expected some gothic aura of decay, something eerie or brooding. Whatever I anticipated, it was not what my daughter and I saw.

First I noticed that the front two of the four giant oaks in the front yard were gone. They had formed an almost perfect square which mirrored the squareness of the house and kept it shaded from the afternoon sun. They had also given us a great deal of grief when the company we hired to lay a new drain field had to deal with the roots. I'd loved those trees, and in our first spring there, had found morel mushrooms growing underneath the northeastern-most one, which was now gone. The missing trees opened up the yard in front of the house, which was bathed in light from the late afternoon sun. The shutters we'd installed that I'd painted a Wedgewood blue were now a burnt orange. I kept my focus off the front steps, noticing instead the splash of fuchsia on the north side of the house, where I'd planted five rhododendrons that grew too slowly to bloom while we lived there. On the south side, I was delighted to see the ancient lilacs still grew over the still-unpaved driveway, forming a natural arbor. It was too late in the season for the lilacs to be in flower, but I could see from the remaining deadheads that it had been an abundant year for them. I wanted simply to pull over, to take our pictures from the side of the road, but Amber urged me to drive around the back of the house. There were no sounds or signs of life, so I listened to her—stupidly.

No sooner than we pulled around back, a man with a can of beer in his hand stepped out of the garage. Shading his eyes from the sun, he approached us with a quizzical expression on his face. Who were we and what did we want? I knew the expression; I'd worn it myself when someone intruded on my privacy. People who choose to live out in the middle of no-damned-where seldom appreciate unexpected company, let alone strangers.

"I help you?" he'd said, probably expecting someone needing directions. That's what most of my interruptions had been: the lost seeking directions.

He was scruffy and scrawny and had the look of someone whose primary source of nutrition was the can of hops soup he held. In fact, I'd known many of his kind and instinctively knew the can was a permanent fixture. Once emptied, it would be immediately replaced by one of its brothers. He reminded me of my younger brother. And like my brother, this guy was alcoholic affability personified.

"We're sorry to bother you," my daughter explained, "but we used to live here. Years ago. This is my mom."

"Hi, Mom," he joked.

But I didn't laugh. He was about my age, certainly not old enough to be calling me his mother.

And then it happened again. That disconnected feeling. The fuzziness around the edges. The blurring of awareness. I could almost hear Tim moaning, "Mama, oh Mama," as he pumped away at me.

I was only vaguely aware of Amber's voice, of the guy with the beer can. I heard her explain what we were doing, and his delighted welcome to explore all we wanted. I know we got out of the car. I know Amber was being her best chatty, charming self. I know he said his name was Sam. I know he accompanied us on our tour, proudly pointing out the alterations he'd made in the house and yard. I know he offered us some beer. I know we declined. I heard Amber's voice, but it seemed muffled, as if she were talking through a pillow. I heard her gush over the treasure trove of happy memories this house held for her. I heard her say things like, "Hey, Mom, do you remember—?" and "Oh my God, I'd forgotten about—" She was excited and happy to revisit this place, and I understood. I understood perfectly.

For her, this house held happy memories.

This had been the first time she'd had her own room. Hers had been the attic room, with a narrow staircase leading up to the hot enclosure with a brick chimney in the center, dormer windows which were painted shut, and slanting ceilings under which even I could not stand except in the very center of the room. But it was hers, her very own, and I worked hard to give it some charm. First, I painted everything a soft white: ceiling, walls, and pine plank floor. Then I stenciled large butterflies in blue and lavender around the entire perimeter and around the intruding chimney. Then I polyurethaned over the floor to preserve the stencil as much as possible. I made simple gathered curtains of a blue and lavender flowered cotton for the two windows, one in front and one in back, and as a cover for her closet which had no door. Then I made her a blue, white, and lavender quilt using the same fabric as the curtains for backing. Amber had loved the A.A. Milne poem "Halfway down the stairs," so I made her quilt in a simple stair-step pattern to go on my great-aunt's spool bed that was then Amber's.

I could hear her telling the guy, telling Sam, about sledding in the driveway in winter and about the path through the back field to her grandparents' house. I heard her tell him about the time we'd camped in the way back, on our own property but far from the conveniences of home.

And I shuddered, then stumbled. Sam's free hand caught me at the elbow, held me steady as I regained my equilibrium. I think I thanked him, but I'm not sure.

Amber kept chatting, animated and happy. Of course she had fond memories of this house. Of course she did. Her happiest school years had been while we lived here, her fondest friendships, sleepovers and Girl Scouts, her doting grandparents a quick walk or bike ride away. Hours of Let's Pretend under the lilacs. Long summer days exploring the four-and-a-half acres on which the house sat. Bouquets of rapidly-wilting dandelions and chicory and devil's paintbrush brought home for me clutched in her or her brothers' precious grubby fists. Is there a finer centerpiece for a kitchen table? For her, this had been a happy home, the last one until she made her own with her husband a decade-and-a-half later.

Before I realized what we were doing, we'd strolled into the front yard. Through a mile or more of cotton batting, I heard Amber explain the indentations in the front porch steps, heard her name my children whose hands had made those indentations in fresh concrete, saw her place her hand over the top one, to see how much she'd grown.

I heard the Sam-man say, "Oh, I see. I'd wondered about them. I get it now. But they're almost gone. Good thing you came when you did."

I thought he meant the exposure to the elements had diminished them somewhat, so I looked at them,

69

focused only on the imprints themselves, squarely on them, willing myself to see only the impressions of my children's hands. And I was startled how insignificant they were. They'd been much deeper back then. Why were they so faint? It hadn't been that long, had it?

"This wasn't the best cement job," Sam said. "Proportion's off. Whoever did it used too much sand. So it ain't holding up too good—"

But Tim had insisted he knew what he was doing. Insisted he knew the exactly right ratio. He swore he knew what he was doing.

"—but that's the good news," Sam continued. "It'll make it easier. I'm putting a deck around the whole house, all four sides, so this'll have to go."

"Wow, that'll be great, won't it, Mom?" Amber gushed, "Mom? Won't it? Hey, Earth to Mom!"

And I have no idea what I said or if I said anything. I have no memory of the next few minutes, until I heard Amber say, "Wow, I'd love that."

"What?" I struggled to regain some sense of awareness. What would Amber love?

"See the inside. See what he's done on the house," she was saying, looking at me expectantly.

"No. Absolutely not," I'd said.

"Mom? Are you all right?"

Somehow I found my voice, or at least a voice. And I was damned if I was setting foot inside that cursed house again.

"No. I think we've intruded on this man's time quite enough. We need to be going," I said, in a tone I hadn't had to use in over a decade. It was my Mom voice, the one that meant "I'm the Mama, and I has spoken." It was not a voice I liked, but it was effective, or had been in the past.

Apparently it still was, as Amber gave a nervous laugh and then acquiesced. "Okay, Mom, whatever you say," she said and headed for the car, pausing only long enough to snap a picture of what little was left of the handprints in the steps.

"Thank you for your kindness," I said to Sam, offering to shake his hand in a formal gesture I've found very effective at establishing authority. And distance.

"No problem," he said. "I enjoyed it. Really. You can come back any time. Really. Any time. We could kick back a few."

He walked us to my car, still chattering inanely.

Amber thanked him as I buckled up and drove out of the driveway, determinedly not looking at the front porch.

"Jesus, Mom, what was that all about?"

"God, I'm sorry, Honey. I didn't even know I still had a Mom card."

"No. I don't mean that. I don't care about that. I thought it was funny. I like seeing the old Mom once in a while. I mean that guy."

"You mean the beer? Not much else to do out in BFE."

"No, Mom. Are you deliberately playing dumb? That guy was, like, poised to strike."

"What are you talking about? He seemed harmless to me."

"Not like that. I mean he never took his eyes off you.

And he kept trying to engage you in conversation. He was like a jug of syrup and you were a short stack."

"Well, thank you very much. Short jokes. And from my own daughter."

"Mom! Focus! You had that guy eating out of your lap and you never gave him the time of day."

"Amber! That is just vulgar."

"But true," she said. Then she began to imitate him, repeating his last words but exaggerating the emphasis and giving him a Southern accent.

"Ya'll COME back now, ya hear. ANY TIME. I'd just love ta see ya again. And again. And again."

She got so involved in her re-invention of his invitation that she didn't notice I'd retreated again into my own thoughts, my own memories.

No, I was not willing to step even one foot back into that house, which had not been so happy for me. To me, that house represented the point at which my life went so terribly wrong. Or maybe it is more that the terribly wrong threads of my life came together here, twisted into a hangman's noose of discontent, dismay, and desperation. That house was my undoing.

Without realizing what I was doing, I turned toward home although there were other houses on our itinerary. Amber didn't notice either, until we were almost there. We then decided to finish the tour another day, another visit, perhaps. We decided to go home and order a pizza for our dinner. For the rest of her visit, a part of me—a large part, I'm afraid—was absent. She sensed that, and it offended her. But the past had arisen and called my name. I had no choice but to respond.

EARLY MIDDLE

D o you believe that houses have souls? Personalities? Energy fields? That it matters little who lives there? That rather than residents shaping the house's character, the house's energy seeps into its residents? That this energy is attracted by the house's address, by the numbers affixed to it? Seems far-fetched on the surface, doesn't it?

But recently, I have become interested in numerology. Although I have never read any convincing support for numerology, house number analysis has seemed creepily accurate.

I have, for example, been happiest in houses with addresses totaling 3: the number of creativity. My house at the time of Amber's visit totaled 8, the number of material success—or a hopeless money pit. The address of the house on Lincoln Road, reduced to a single digit by adding the individual ones, totaled 2, the number of duality, of the occult, of madness. I didn't know numerology back then and probably wouldn't have put any stock in such foolishness. Not back then. A smart investment is a smart investment, and I knew this house was a smart investment. With a little work—okay, okay, a hell of a lot of hard work—that house could easily double in value in just a few years.

Have you heard the saying, generally attributed to JFK, that some people see things as they are and say, "Why?" while others see things as they could be and say, "Why not?" Well, I see things as they really are and as they could be, and ask, "How?" This is both a blessing and a curse, as I am often alone in my vision, others shaking their heads or shying away from the reality, blind to the possibility.

So I saw what this drab cinder block house could be. Tim was no work shirk and had many of the skills we would need to accomplish a rehab, and I had the vision. The first thing to go was that nightmare porch, which presented a very real hazard, as the kids, forbidden from playing anywhere on, under, or near it, were quite naturally irresistibly drawn to it.

I'd never done anything on that scale, but one day the itch got too strong and I started pulling up the floor boards. I started with Tim's crowbar but found the wood to be so rotten that I could pull it up more easily with my gloved hands. Plank by plank it came up and I dragged the old wood to the road, thinking that we'd probably need to burn it to get rid of it.

The floor, the steps, the railings all came off and down as if that were exactly what they wanted for themselves. Perhaps it was. I was amazed at how efficiently I tore that sucker apart, singlehandedly. In mere hours, there was a huge pile of old wood by the road, and nothing was left across the front of the house but the supporting pillars and the roof. Tim laughed when he saw it.

Then he went for his circular saw, climbed up on the roof of the house, and cut the supports. There was a rather anticlimactic, muted crash as the roof came down. The saw had made more noise. Tim helped me drag the remains to the road, and we went inside for quick showers and a hearty meal. As we discussed the best means of disposal of the defunct porch wood, we heard a car horn from the road. Investigating, we found a guy with a flatbed truck parked in the entrance of the driveway.

"Mind if I take this wood?" he asked, after the fact. He'd already begun to load it.

"I'll pay you if you want."

Tim and I looked at each other in disbelief.

"Make you a deal," said Tim. "I won't charge you for it if you don't charge me to haul it away."

I laughed and headed back into the house. I'd done enough physical labor for one day, but Tim helped him load it up. Later Tim told me that the guy said he used it for firewood to heat his house in winter. That he was almost never down this quiet country road, but for some reason had turned down it that day. Unbelievable. All I could think was that it must have been meant to be.

So the front of the house became a blank slate on which we could inscribe our own vision. The best part of all was how much light could stream through the front windows—the living room and the boys' bedroom. It seemed like an augury of happiness and hope. If it was, it was a false one. A big fat lie. There was to be damn little happiness for me there, and hope was already trickling away.

Whether it was the influence of the house itself or something in Tim that he'd kept in check before, I'll never know. God knows, it's too late to investigate. The previous owner of the house had been an abusive, alcoholic slacker. My folks had known him and his wife.

She was a quiet, unassuming beige woman who seemed resigned to her lot in life. Her lot was her husband. He would get some grand scheme for making lots of money for very little work, go gangbusters for a while, then lose interest when the "very little" work became "considerable" work or the bottle demanded his attention. So the garage was partially insulated with an ugly orange spray-on foam he'd toyed with some years before. He'd tried to teach himself to use the foam by spraying some here, some there, with no apparent plan. Then he'd gotten tired of it, perhaps because it was clearly not going to be all that effortless. So he switched to something else, leaving the mess where it fell.

My folks told me, too, about the way he treated his wife, emotionally battering her, insulting and ridiculing her, calling her vile names right in front of them, then quickly switching to a grinning, pseudo-charming smile for their benefit. They'd heard stories, too, about bruises and broken bones, about late-night ambulance calls, about her habitual wearing of long-sleeved shirts and long dresses, even in the summer. So my folks discouraged his attempts at neighborly visits until he finally gave up and left them alone.

It was he who decided to sell the house, who decided that they could make good money with very little work by driving truck across the country. Without the expense of a house, without the responsibility of real estate, all the money they made would be theirs. Code for 'his,' of course. For booze. And she meekly did as she was told. They sold everything and off they went. A credit union handled my house payments, and I never saw either one of them again. No loss to me.

I like to think that, freed from the influence of the house, maybe he changed back into whatever he'd been that drew her to him in the first place. Because that's the only reason I can think of to explain why she stayed with someone like that: he once had been a good guy, maybe a great guy, who had inexplicably changed, perhaps when they moved into that house. And maybe she stayed because she'd loved that great guy he had been so much that she could never quite give up even the tiniest shred of hope that he might return someday, might show up on her porch with an armload of daffodils. That's what I told myself. I couldn't stand the thought that she'd stayed because on some level she had convinced herself, or life had convinced her, that she actually deserved such treatment, that in fact she was so contemptible that derision, scorn, and abuse were comfortable, were what she had coming. No, no, no. Unthinkable. Unacceptable.

My fantasy of a reverse metamorphosis from a

person of value and worth to an unreliable, mean, ugly slug of a man was preferable. Besides, I had based my fantasy on Tim's transformation—and my own.

We threw ourselves into the many demands of the rehab. Tim had told me he had a heart condition, a murmur or something. I didn't pay much attention to his claim that he could "pop off at any minute" because he didn't seem to, either. He over-did everything. Everything. He ate too much, worked too much, smoked too much, and drank too much.

By hand with a shovel, he turned over the soil for a sizable vegetable garden. Set back maybe fifty feet from the house, it would yield an abundance of tomatoes, zucchini, cabbage, beans and kohlrabi he planned to plant. Stripping his shirt from his odd, skinny, flat body, he would work for hours, turning and turning the soil. I suggested we rent a tiller, or buy one if he planned to do this every year, but he scoffed at the idea.

"Lazy man's way," he insisted. "This is the way it's been done forever. Good enough for me."

The sweat that ran in rivulets from his body must have helped fertilize the soil, as his first crop was staggering. He had to haul bushelsful to distribute among his co-workers after I'd frozen as much as our new upright freezer would hold and we'd shared with my parents and neighbors.

His body darkened rapidly in the sun with never a burn. He said it was his Native American blood, that he was part Cherokee, but when I asked for specifics, for a clue to his claimed heritage, he clammed up. Same thing happened with the John Muir thing.

He claimed to be descended from the famous American naturalist, but refused to share details. For his birthday, I was able to track down a first edition of one of Muir's books. He'd been delighted, one of the few times he showed any genuine pleasure.

But what his link was to Muir, I could not discover. His mother's side? His father's? I could get nothing from him about any family information other than both his parents were dead. He said he had an older brother, but never spoke of him, never called or visited him. That I knew of, at least. Tim never heard from this phantom brother either and I never saw a photo of him. Tim was an enigma for the most part, and I didn't pry any further.

I respected his work ethic and his stamina. I envied him his metabolism. I appreciated his financial support. But I never loved him. I refused to speak to him about marriage, as my parents kept insisting. They saw our living together as sinful, as shameful, and were afraid Scott would find out and sue for custody. Clearly only an unfit mother would live with a man she was not married to. I understood their concerns came from my dad's own past, and I could not get them to understand that times had changed, the laws had changed. Living with Tim, or more accurately, letting him live with us, did not make me an unfit mother. Besides, Scott hadn't even seen the kids for over two years, hadn't bothered to send them so much as a birthday card. If he protested, I knew all I'd have to do is remind him I'd settled for the least possible child support, but it would be an easy matter to ask for a raise. Which I'd be forced to do if I had to support us all by myself. Scott understood moneyspeak.

And as well, I didn't really want Tim's name, didn't want to be permanently fused to him. So I kept telling my parents that one glitch or another prevented his divorce from going through, that there was no point in discussing marriage to a married man. That wasn't exactly a lie; it was just not the whole truth. The whole truth was that we were a convenience to each other; our individual needs matched as neatly as the yin-yang symbol, but there was no grand passion. No genuine affection, even. Which makes it all worse, I suppose. We had yoked ourselves together out of convenience and mutual need, so it wasn't even a crime of passion.

In a way, it makes more sense for a passionate love to turn into passionate hate. The flip side of the same coin, or further end of the same spectrum which might not even be linear but circular, doubling back on itself. We all know people who've remarried their ex-spouse. As deeply as we love, we are capable of hating. But there was no real hate, either. It wasn't hate that drove me. Just as I hadn't loved him, I hadn't hated him, either. He was just there like someone else's taste in wallpaper that isn't your taste, but is still in good enough condition to postpone replacement. He was just there, pulling his own weight and not intruding on the way I chose to pull mine. At least that's the way it was before we moved into the new house.

One of the major projects on the house was to reconstruct some kind of front porch. We had not been able to use the rotten one, and it had probably been a very long time since anyone had. The circle drive went behind the house, so it was the back door that we used. There was not even a walkway to the unused front door, but the house looked odd with nothing there but the door floating four feet off the ground. We discussed alternatives and finally decided on a simple set of wide steps leading up to a brief landing.

Tim, of course, decided to build it himself. He dismissed my suggestion to use pre-mixed concrete, or to have a concrete company deliver a load after he built the forms. One day he came home with a large metal-lined trough for mixing the cement and sand and did the work himself. All but the cap, that is.

First he dug a trench around the area over which he intended to build the porch. He said we couldn't just pour onto the level ground. The porch needed footers. Then he bought half-inch plywood sheets and staked them up nearly a foot apart. He explained that the plywood would come off after the concrete set. He set the forms for the steps, too, a good six feet wide. It took most of the second summer we were in the house as it was a huge job and he could work on it only sporadically; his garden took most of his time. Tilling, planting, weeding, and de-bugging demanded his time at home, but he was home less and less.

He claimed he was asked to work overtime, double shifts sometimes. I had never seen his pay stubs, so had no idea how much of the truth he told. But he started to come home reeking of beer, and more than once one of the kids found cigarette butts with lipstick on them in the ashtray of the back seat. I couldn't even fake outrage or disappointment. I just didn't want him to bring home any nasty diseases, so I began to avoid his attentions. His personality began to change, too. Not that he'd had much personality to begin with, but at least he'd been amenable, civil to me and my kids. Occasionally even playing with them. The bike race with Amber, for example. Or taking us all picnicking or fishing.

The previous owner of the Lincoln Road house had been a smarmy alcoholic ne're-do-well, and it seemed as if Tim were being metamorphosed into the same. He drank more, he smoked more, and stayed out later and later. But that had nothing to do with me and my kids, so I tried to ignore it. What I couldn't ignore was his tone when he spoke to any of us. Whatever I suggested was dismissed with a contemptuous tone, and the kids were an increasing irritation to him. He'd complain about and to them and began calling them names, began ridiculing them for, apparently, the audacity of just being kids. He seemed to expect them to work as hard as we did instead of playing. He started shoving them out of his way or viciously kicking a neglected toy out of his way. He began to refer to my kids as "those little shits" or "the shitheads." I hadn't loved him, maybe, but I'd respected him. Not any longer.

One payday morning, when I usually did the weekly grocery shopping, he was not there when I woke up. On a hunch, I drove down to a particularly scruffy bar a few miles away. Sure enough, his car was there. I was damned if I was going to go in there and drag him out, but when he finally got home, I confronted him.

"Don't you think this is a bit ridiculous?" I asked as he stumbled over the threshold. "If you don't want to come home, don't come home. If you don't want to be here anymore, just move out. Just get it over with."

But he'd looked blearily in my general direction and muttered, "Don't know what you're talking 'bout. Just wanna go ta bed. Pulled a double shift." His words were slurred all together. From at least six feet away, the reek of the beer he'd consumed assaulted my nose.

"Pulled a double bender, you mean," I shot back. But my years of working in bars taught me one thing for sure: You cannot reason with a drunk. Drunks and crazies, there is just no point in wasting your breath. So he crawled into bed, and I went about my day.

Suddenly the porch moved up on my priorities list. Tim's time in my house was running out. He'd be leaving us sooner or later, and I did not want to get stuck with the uncapped landing. If I were lucky, he'd cap it before he moved on to his next unsuspecting victim.

So, on that day, I moved a number of wheelbarrow loads of rubble from behind the garage where the previous owners had apparently started their own private landfill. Not much work had been done on the porch, not for months, and I'd started to worry that the kids wouldn't be able to resist the temptation to play in the vault-like concrete wall. Tim kept putting off and putting off capping the damn thing, the last thing that needed doing.

I'd watched much of the work Tim had done, understood how to set a form; how to mix the concrete to the right proportions of sand, cement, and water; when to remove the forms, not too early, not too late. But filling the pit with concrete would have been too expensive and too time-consuming. So we'd started filling the pit with the rubble from behind the garage. Tim had set up a temporary ramp against the steps, so we could run the wheelbarrow up the ramp and just dump it. But it was so discouraging to see how little a nearly top-heavy load would amount to in the bottom of the pit. I lost count of the loads and finally had to quit when my strength gave out.

Like many people—maybe you, too—for most of my life, I've had a problem with not giving myself enough credit for my accomplishments. Whatever I do is not enough for my inner judge, jury, and executioner. Not ever good enough, not deep enough, not high enough, not smooth enough, not fast enough, not ever anything enough. Instead of giving myself some credit, some appreciation, some encouraging words (as I would easily have done for a friend, family member, or even a total stranger), I just beat myself up for not doing better. At least I used to do this; I've been trying very hard for the last few years to change this. I've tried to be as supportive of myself as I am of others. I would never in a million years speak to another person as harshly as I speak to myself. But remember, it is only fairly recently I've tried to apply a reverse golden rule: Do not do to yourself what you would not do to anyone else. On the day I'm describing, it was still the same old me.

I'd wanted to accomplish so much more. Now I realize it was an unrealistic goal—to fill the whole damn pit so Tim could get it capped before he moved out, before I kicked him out—but I'd filled only about a foot or so with the broken bricks and concrete chunks and cinders from the coal burning furnace the house must've had at some time. There were also broken bottles and jars and rusted cans in the rubbish heap, so we had to be careful not to get cut as we loaded shovelful after shovelful into wheelbarrowful after wheelbarrowful. Only a foot or so of rubble and my back, shoulders, arms and legs were screaming in protest. Now I know enough to say "enough" and "good enough is good enough." But back then, my physical limitations dictated my decisions.

Disappointed and disgusted with myself, I went inside to find Tim at the table—a picnic table he'd made because I didn't want a traditional kitchen table. He was busily sketching something. As I entered, he made the few final strokes.

"There," he said in a tone that implied a childlike, "Ta-da!"

"What do you think about this?" he asked.

I was shocked to see what he'd been doing: planning a second story addition which would nearly double the house's square footage, with three upstairs bedrooms and a second full bath. His plan changed the roof to a mansard style, which was a perfect fit to the four-square existing first floor. With the roomy upstairs bedrooms, each of the kids could have his or her own room, which I knew the boys would love. Our existing bedroom off the kitchen he'd converted on paper to a spacious laundry room and pantry so I wouldn't have to go downstairs into the creepy, damp basement. It was a terrific plan. But I was confused.

"What are you doing?" I asked.

"Maybe if we had more room to spread out, we wouldn't get on each other's nerves so much," he said.

And I didn't know what to say, so I said nothing. What was all this about? Why now? Did he have no memory of our earlier argument? I'd already started making plans for getting a job, for moving him out.

"I'll call a contractor tomorrow," he said. "Start getting some quotes."

"What about the porch? The front steps?"

"No point in paying for what I can do myself," he said. "I'll get it done."

This was the start of a very confusing period in our life. Tim would go to work, eat and sleep, day after day for weeks, then suddenly be joking and playful and energetic. He would snap and snarl, then suddenly be soft-spoken and charming. Well, maybe not charming exactly, but sort of deliberately civil and thoughtful. I never knew what mood he would be in or how long it would last. And we would have the strangest arguments until I learned to recognize the signs of an upcoming one and sidestep it.

For example, he worked, coincidentally, at the same factory as Scott, but they didn't know each other; thousands of people worked there on three different shifts around the clock, so this was no surprise. But one day he came home and said he'd finally seen my ex. A co-worker had pointed him out.

"Tall guy, right?"

"Tall enough," I answered, "Five ten or eleven."

"No, he isn't." Tim scoffed. "He's a good six-four."

"Scott? No way."

"Yes, he is. And long hair, right?"

"Last I saw, yes. Past his shoulders."

"Yep. Dirty blond, right?"

Now, it was possible that Scott had bleached his hair, but highly unlikely. He had glossy, nearly black hair of which he was exceedingly vain.

"No. Black. Long black hair. And he isn't quite six foot."

Suddenly Tim's face contorted as he screamed into mine. "Don't you fucking lie to me. I guess I know your ex when I see him."

This was so unexpected, so irrational, that I had nothing to say. In fact, it was all I could do not to laugh in his face. What the hell was all of this?

I don't know if I've ever been truly afraid of anyone before. I've been in some dicey places, some hairy moments that could easily have gone badly, but somehow a calmness had overtaken me, had commanded the moment, and I've managed to avoid some of the situations other women I knew had been subjected to. Maybe my refusal to cower, to grovel, or even to acknowledge the danger has deflected the violent impulses I've sensed impending. Or maybe I've just been lucky. But there was something new, or newly unleashed, in Tim that threw me off balance. His mood changes unnerved me. And I think he knew it.

One day as I had just come up the basement steps from changing out a load of laundry, he suddenly loomed over me in a threatening posture, his head lowered, his shoulders hunched, his fists clenched. He didn't say a word, but I could literally feel the evil energy emanating from him. I knew with absolute certainty that he meant to shove me down the stairs.

For what? Why? I did not know, or care. Somehow I remained absolutely calm—and said his name. "Tim," I said. "Excuse me." And I moved gradually but purposefully forward.

His head shook almost imperceptibly, as yours might when you realize you've been woolgathering instead of paying attention. Then the look in his eyes changed, the energy between us changed, and he meekly moved aside.

Another time, he'd been working in the garden, digging and digging, turning the soil for days. Then he summoned me out to see what he'd accomplished. He did that often, seeking approval, seeking appreciation, as anyone might. But there was something different in his tone on this occasion. It was not a request. It was a demand, slow, low, and threatening.

"Come here, Edwina. I want to show you something."

And suddenly I became alarmed on a very deep, very primal level. There was something in his tone, something in his steady level gaze, and something in the way his jaw muscle twitched that absolutely convinced me that Tim intended to kill me, to bury me out there with the seed potatoes. Great fertilizer, I suppose, but I wasn't wisecracking then. You know those cold sweats you've read about when someone is truly terrified? They are real, not just a literary convention, not a cliché. And I had them. And I had something else, too: an absolute certainty that if I showed the slightest flicker of intimidation, he would become enraged, become unmanageable. So I did go out to his garden, but it took every fragment of willpower to do so—and to appear calm. This I knew: I must remain calm.

Tim stared at me, locked my gaze in his, as he explained his plan for that year's garden. His knuckles were white where he clutched the shovel. His eyes were dark pits of inexplicable anger, of resentment, of threat, but his words were so innocuous. Here there would be corn, there would be tomatoes, over there kohlrabi. Mix up the placement, he explained, so as not to deplete the soil. Each of the types of plants sucked specific nutrients from the soil. You have to change their beds every year. Even if you fertilize, he explained, absolutely deadpan.

And I matched his dark gaze, only God knows how, as inside my mind I was making a run for my parent's house and screaming bloody murder. But somehow I knew in my bones that a response such as that would be my undoing, would trigger exactly what I feared. Then the words just came out of my mouth, the just-right words, the perfect words, in the perfect tone, without my conscious effort. I praised him. Profusely.

"I am so impressed, Tim. You have done such an amazing job out here. I am so grateful, Tim, for your hard work."

That was all. And the snap happened again. His head did that little almost imperceptible twitch, and he broke his gaze, began to look around the garden as if he'd never seen it before, didn't know how he got there, even. He began to look at the things he was talking about instead of staring intently at me. Or through me. Past me. Post-me.

He did call a contractor who came and gave us an amazingly reasonable quote for the frame-in. Tim intended to do the finish work himself. He said he could, and I had no reason to doubt him. But I stalled the project. I don't remember what excuses I offered. Start in the spring? Wait for the new drain field to be done? Wait for his tax return? What I do know is that I did not tell the truth. I did not say what I absolutely knew to be the truth: You aren't going to be here to do the finish work, and I will not be able to make enough money on my own to afford to hire it done. I could not have foretold how he would leave, but expected him to leave me the way he'd left his wife: a simple segue into another woman's bed—and life. He would stay out later and later, longer and longer, until one day he'd just be gone. And I'd be safe. Alone, but safe. Dirt poor, but safe.

I also expected his nastiness to remain aimed at me. But I was wrong. And I can't forgive myself for not seeing it coming.

Every now and then, when what I came to think of as the Good Tim would wax expansive, he'd insist on all of us piling into the car and driving the hour and a half to his favorite fishing spot at the tip of the thumb. Even from outer space, the state of Michigan is recognizable as a left mitten. If you hold out your left hand, palm away from you, you can locate Grindstone City at the tip of your outstretched thumb. It wasn't much of a city anymore, but had been a thriving town where grindstones were made—thus the name. Of course, many of the rejected, neglected smaller grindstones have been pilfered away as garden art and lawn ornaments. People will steal anything they can lift, just for the hell of it. Have you noticed that? Fortunately, some of the grindstones are too large to be hoisted away, even with help, so at the shoreline you can still perch on a gigantic grindstone to fish. And Tim loved to do just that.

We'd drive up there early on a Saturday or a Sunday. Tim would fish, silent and focused; the kids would clamber over the rocks and grindstones, and I'd watch them play as I made flower garlands of dandelions, daisies, or chicory, depending on what was in bloom. For the most part, it was as if we were two separate parties at the shore: Tim by himself, me with my kids. But our last day at Grindstone City was different. On this day, Tim was clearly aware of our presence, angrily aware of our presence. He snapped at the kids and me. Every movement, every sound irritated him. He criticized and insulted and scolded and sneered. Then Ashley made the mistake of getting too close. Tim's ire was suddenly focused entirely on him. He said Ashley was old enough to learn to fish. He decided to teach him.

I haven't told you much about the kids yet, partly out of deliberate reticence, a desire to keep them out of this particular picture as much as possible, to protect them if I can from the inevitable repercussions when the truth surfaces about what I did—and what I intend to do. But you do need to understand that Ashley, even more than a normal 7-year-old boy child, was a walking, talking fidget. He did not even sleep still, but twitched and tossed even in his deepest dream states. And he had no interest in anything that required him to be still, had no interest in fishing.

If he'd said, "Hey, Tim, teach me to fish," that would've been one thing. But for Tim to say, "Ash, boy, come 'ere. It's high time you learned to fish," was just an engraved, hand-delivered invitation to disaster. The more Tim insisted on Ashley's compliance, the less Ashley complied. He didn't want to touch the bait, worms Tim had dug up in the garden. Ashley couldn't get the hang of casting. He would not or could not wait patiently in silent anticipation for something that was simply not happening. It was not fun for Ashley. It was not fun for Tim. And it sure as hell wasn't fun for me as I saw the darkness come over Tim's face and his jaw muscle start to twitch.

As I watched them, still trying to keep an eye on the other two kids, I became convinced that Tim would harm my son that day. That he would push him into the crevices of the rocks and grindstones or into the water. Paranoia or premonition? Who knows? But as Ashley turned to step away from Tim, his fishing pole trailing its line, all but forgotten in his hand, Tim lunged at him, pure hatred in his eyes. But Ashley's attention had shifted, something off to his right had caught his attention, and he hopped quickly to investigate so that Tim, trying to cuff him, missed and lost his own balance. He skidded down the rock, cursing as he went. He ended up in the water, which was not deep at that spot. As Tim dragged himself out of the water, his face contorted in rage. I did not know what to do, how to protect my son.

"Are you all right, Tim?" I asked, feigning a concern I did not feel. "Are you hurt? What happened?"

Of course, I knew what had happened; I saw the whole thing. But I was trying to divert his anger. I repeated my question several times, trying with everything in me to remain calm and sound sincere. It had worked before and it might again.

It did. After a few tense moments when I knew it could have gone either way, Tim looked at me, a puzzled and disconcerted expression on his face.

"Don't know. Guess I slipped on the wet rocks. I guess I wasn't paying attention."

"You're bleeding," I said, noticing his scraped hands. "Let me put some ice on that."

I pulled a clump of ice cubes from the ice chest packed with soda and beer. The scrapes were superficial, of course, and Tim took over the job of icing them down for himself. He didn't say another word to Ashley, and I stupidly thought that was the end of it, that I'd succeeded in diverting Tim's anger away from my son. We left after that. I'd brought changes of clothing for the kids in case they got wet, but hadn't anticipated that Tim would, so he had to stay in his wet ones, which must have been uncomfortable. But he said nothing about it. The whole way home, Tim was silent, but that was not uncommon. His silences were normal for him, and not an indication of a smoldering anger, not necessarily an augury of disaster. We even stopped on the way home for cones at a quaintly restored ancient general store-turned-ice-cream-parlor. We pulled into the driveway just at sunset, usually my favorite time of the day.

The kids had fallen asleep in the back seat, slumped onto each other as they never would have while awake. Kids need their own space, have you noticed that? Tim silently stepped out from behind the wheel and went around the car to the back door on my side, the door against which Ashley still slept. And again, I thought nothing of this. We often carried sleeping children into the house and lay them fully clothed on their beds. I have always hated waking a sleeping baby. Amber was 10, Ashley was 7, and Jason was 2, but they were still my babies. They are still. Tim opened the back door as I stepped out of mine. I expected him to hand Jason into my arms and then to carry first Ashley, then Amber into the house. So I was horrified when, instead of gently extracting him, Tim dragged Ashley out of the car by his hair, dumping him in the dirt of the driveway. I was even more horrified as he began viciously to kick the still-sleeping Ashley with the steel-toed work boots he always wore.

"Stop it!" I screamed at Tim and tried to lunge at him. "Stop it! What the hell do you think you are doing? Stop it!" But Tim aimed two more kicks at my son before he stopped. "You keep out of this, you stupid fucking bitch. He knows what he did. Him and me, we understand each other."

Then he stalked into the house and slammed the door behind him as I sat in the dirt wiping away Ashley's tears and trying to calm the other two at the same time.

And that's when it all changed for good.

The next morning, Tim behaved as if nothing had happened. But when I looked at him, it was as if I'd never seen him before. I hadn't noticed before that his head was too small for his body, grotesquely too small. I hadn't noticed that his protruding Adam's apple, linked with his perpetual slouch and hooked nose, made him resemble the contemptible turkey buzzards we occasionally saw in the road squabbling over a particularly tasty bit of road kill. Carrion eaters. We need them, but they are ugly, ugly, ugly. Tim was now incredibly ugly to me, contemptible, vile. I wanted him gone.

But just gone, you understand. Just out of our lives. I read once that if you tell someone they look like a person with cancer, that he or she will, in fact, have cancer within a year. Well, that's pure B.S. If that were true, we wouldn't need divorce, would we? You can plant the seed of suggestion for a headache, maybe, or an upset stomach. But not cancer. If I could have willed it so, Tim would never have awoken the next morning.

I slept on the sofa that night, the night after he attacked my son, and vowed never again to share a room with him, much less a bed. As I stood at the foot of my antique brass bed and looked down on his still-sleeping scrawny body sprawled across my sheets, I decided to side-step any unpleasant scenes. I'd simply pack up all his things and put them out on the porch, set them outside the teepee in a gesture his alleged Native American blood would recognize. Then suddenly I noticed something that changed everything.

There were burn holes in my sheets. More burn holes, although he'd promised not to smoke in bed any more since I awoke one morning to a half-smoked cigarette and black-rimmed holes where he'd damn near incinerated us as we slept. The power of nicotine was so strong over him that even as he slept he would light up, take a few drags, then let the cigarette fall from his sleeping hand. If the sheets had been all-cotton instead of cotton-poly blend, they would have ignited instead of melted. As every sheet set I owned had burn holes in them, I decided I needed some new ones. And I preferred all cotton.

I stood staring at the burn holes, envisioning it all: I could see the kids going off with their grandparents, perhaps to church. I could see myself lighting one of Tim's cigarettes, handling it gingerly so no identifiable prints could be lifted. I could see myself flicking the burning cigarette into the bed, into the brand new all-cotton sheets, maybe even encouraging the flame a little. I could see myself leaving the room, shutting the door behind me and going, maybe, to the grocery store, stopping at the fruit market, maybe even a rummage sale or two, taking my time. I could see the billows of smoke from miles away, hear the sirens, see the gathered firefighting and rescue vehicles as I neared the driveway. I could even see the shocked expression on my own face as I saw the blackened ruin of my house and the black-vinyl-draped stretcher as they removed Tim's skinny, ugly, lifeless, useless piece-of-shit body. I could see the blackened fragments of my first patchwork quilt, my favorite so far, the one I kept on my bed for everyday use so I could see and appreciate my handiwork.

No. Not my quilt. But if I first removed all the items that I valued, I would arouse suspicion. Maybe if I had the quilt hanging on the line? Maybe I'd washed it? It would still get smoky, maybe even singed, but would be intact. Nope. That just wouldn't work. I couldn't risk my quilt.

I'd just kick him out. Getting him to go would be the trick. I sensed that if I wanted him to go, he wouldn't; if I begged him to stay, he would. Ignoring him might work, though.

And if I were going to be on my own again, the first order of the day would be a job. Other than the demolition skills I'd learned, I was still as under-employable as ever. Almost. I could still shlep drinks, and I'd left Tom & Jerry's under cordial circumstances. Money is money, and a job is a job.

All I had to do was walk in the door. Magda, a daytime regular three years before, was still in her assigned barstool. She took one look at me and shouted, "Eddie? Are you looking for a job? Talk about timing. Tom needs you. Now."

I started three days later. The crowd had changed again, this time an older, more economically established one, so the tips had changed, too. I calculated and re-calculated my potential income. I would make it. House payment, car payment, utilities, groceries if we ate a lot of macaroni and cheese. Fortunately, my kids have always loved macaroni and cheese.

But I had to wait for just the right moment to tell Tim to move out. I wanted to time the request carefully, as I now knew he was dangerous, and I didn't want to risk inflaming him (no pun intended). I ignored him as much as possible, even when he made the pathetically predictable reconciliation overtures after the fateful Grindstone City trip. Of course, he knew my buttons: my kids and my house. So he lavished attention on both. The two older kids' guards were up, but little Jason, who was born trusting and forgiving, responded to Tim's attentions. And the house was receptive, too.

Tim started working on the front steps again. Sort of. What he did made no sense to me, but I couldn't question his reasoning without breaking my self-imposed reign of silence. He erected the sides of the cap from plywood. Then he started to haul up more of the rubble, but didn't put it directly into the pit. He started a second heap of rubble right there in the front yard beside the first. I ached to challenge his logic. Why shovel it twice? Why not dump it directly into the built-up pit? Then he started a third heap. It was all I could do to keep silent, to continue to ignore him. But I was damned if I would give him the satisfaction of my curiosity or confusion. And then there was the issue of his work habits.

He'd work like a demon, then stop suddenly, take a shower and leave the house, heading north if it were time for him to leave for work, or south in the direction of the bar. If he were home, he was sleeping or working in the garden or at the porch.

Of course, I hated the mess he left in the front yard, hated that it looked like a half-finished, half-assed job. Then it occurred to me that to passers-by (not that there were many on any given day) it would look as if he'd been working diligently on the project and had perhaps at this very moment stepped away for a break, a cold beer or a cigarette. Maybe they would think, "Gee, what a hard worker that guy is. You should've seen the house before he started fixing it up."

And then I got a more sinister thought. Maybe it was closer to being filled in than I imagined. Remember, it was a good-sized construction, maybe six feet wide by five feet deep by four feet high with walls a good eight inches thick that he'd poured himself, load by load, in the good old fashioned way that he preferred. There were three deep steps leading to the top, and on each step he'd had the kids press their hands into the nearly-set concrete. Amber's on the top step, Ashley's on the middle, Jason's on the bottom, in appropriate birth order. At the time, I'd thought that charming. Now I thought of headstones, tombstones, grave markers. I thought how tidily we four would fit into that pit, how easily the rubble would fill the pit the rest of the way, especially now that it was conveniently located. The third side of the plywood form was already cut and ready to place so the cap could be poured.

How many wheelbarrows full of wet concrete would it take to cap our crypt? How long would it be before we were missed? How would he explain our disappearance? My parents lived next door, for crying out loud. How did he expect to get away with it? The bastard. The filthy, ugly, murderous bastard. I hated him even more, even after I'd snapped out of it. What bizarre thoughts. What on earth put such evil thoughts into my head? Never in my life had I indulged in such ugly fantasies. Fantasies aplenty, but never these ugly ones. Such mundane fantasies. Fantasies of winning the lottery and building a house of my own with my own hands, maybe one of those cordwood log houses. I'd read several poorly-written and obviously self-published books about alternative house building, and the cordwood log seemed most feasible. Fantasies of dream vacations, Hawaii, maybe, with my kids, watching them playing on the beach. Fantasies of a new kitchen with maybe marble counter tops. Fantasies of grocery shopping with no consideration of price per serving or price per pound or price at all. Smoked salmon? Jumbo shrimp? Kiwis out of season? No problem. Fantasies of never having to stretch another seventy-nine cents into a dollar. Even as my marriage to Scott disintegrated, my fantasies were mundane: that he would suddenly, inexplicably, come home one day and see me, see us, with fresh eyes, with loving eyes, would recognize the ineffable value of a devoted wife and healthy, happy kids, and a decent-paying job. Would want me again.

What the hell was going on? I thought again of the house. These thoughts only surfaced when I was inside the house. In the yard, even just out on the back porch sitting with my second cup of coffee, I was fine. I thought of what to make for dinner or what pattern quilt to attempt next or what color to paint the new shutters. Was it possible that a house—that this house, in fact—could exert an evil influence over its inhabitants? It seemed too far-fetched. I believed in evil, even then. Who does not who watches the news on TV? Children murdering their parents; parents murdering their children; cruelty to animals; greed and selfishness in the extreme. Who could not believe that evil exists?

But I believed that evil exists in the hearts and minds of human beings. I did not, still do not, believe in a personified Devil with cloven hoofs and a tail. The Devil was not making me paranoid. And the Devil was not making Tim act so erratically. I've already told you about learning that, in numerology, the duality inherent in houses with addresses that reduce to the number 2 can cause mental unbalance, can cause psychic disruptions. But at the time, all I could come up with was that I was going nuts. Plain and simple: nuts.

Why the hell would Tim want me dead? It was illogical. He stood to gain absolutely nothing by my disappearance or death. I had no insurance policies with him as the named beneficiary. His name was not on the house or my car; besides, he had his own car. Conversely, his death would not benefit me, either. I'd stumbled across some of his paperwork and discovered his wife's name was still on the policy he had through the shop. She was the only one who might stand to gain anything by his death. I wondered if she'd mourn him. Then another terrifying thought occurred to my already exhausted brain.

What about her? Debra. His wife. With a shudder

that sent goosebumps from my scalp to the hairs on my toes, I realized I'd never met her. I'd never heard her voice. Or seen her handwriting. She'd never called him, never sent him anything, never had him served with divorce papers. I'd never even seen a picture of her. Or their baby, the one who had died in infancy.

According to Tim, that is. According to Tim, she was now romantically involved elsewhere and had no time or interest in his whereabouts or activities. According to Tim. According to Tim. Dear God in Heaven. Reality, according to Tim, might well be a total work of fiction. I'd never asked to meet her, to see her, to know anything about her at all. I'd accepted everything he'd told me as fact. I'd sought no verification. No evidence. For all I knew—Oh Dear God—for all I knew, there was another concrete porch on another house. For all I knew, there were other sets of hands impressed in concrete steps. For all I knew. Oh Shit! His parents! He said they were dead. Were they? How'd they die? Could he prove it? Where were they buried? Who the hell was this man, anyway?

In other words, I scared myself half to death. Tim wouldn't have to bother trying to do me in. At this rate, I'd do it myself. Death by morbid, over-active, obsessive-compulsive imagination.

The only way to stop my train of thought was to get out of the house, get into the outdoors, into the sun. So I did.

I put on my work gloves and started loading rubble into the wheelbarrow. My folks had taken the kids to the Children's Zoo and planned to feed them before they brought them home, so I paid no attention to the time until the first mosquitoes' buzz at sundown drove me back inside. The rubble pile behind the garage did not seem much depleted, but the ones in the front yard had grown. I'd done enough hauling and lifting that my muscles had strengthened, and the physical labor seemed exhilarating rather than exhausting. I'd barely finished a quick supper of two fried eggs, over easy, and an English muffin when my folks pulled in. My dad helped me carry the exhausted younger two into the house. Amber dragged in leaning against my mom. We exchanged small talk as I pajama-ed the boys and Amber brushed her teeth.

"Where's Tim?" my dad asked.

Suddenly I realized that he'd never come home. And I realized that I hadn't even noticed and did not care.

"I don't know," I said. "He hasn't come home yet. Maybe he pulled some overtime."

My mom's sniff of disapproval was about as subtle as an avalanche. "And he didn't call you?"

"I've been outside, working in the yard. Maybe he tried."

They exchanged a significance-laden glance, then my dad cleared his throat and said, "Honey, we've been meaning to talk to you—"

"—about Tim," finished my mom. They always spoke this way, in sentence fragments shuffled into each other. "We really don't mean to keep—"

"—interfering. But you know how we feel about—"

"—you two living together. And we really think—"

I interrupted. "I know, I know. You think we should

107

get married. But I've told you—"

"No!" they said simultaneously, startling me and themselves.

"No," said my dad. "We think, actually, that you should—"

"—get rid of him," finished my mom.

And they looked at me, not saying another word, for a good ten seconds. Ten seconds doesn't sound like much, but, depending on the circumstances, can be a very long time. It is approximately ten heartbeats. Go ahead and try it. Feel your heart beat and count out ten of them, imagine you are in the middle of a conversation. See? A long time.

Then I said, "Okay, but what do I do with the body?"

That old family joke. Said hundreds of times by one or another of us. Just a flippant, smart-assed remark. A quick comeback. Clever. Witty. Off-handed. Predictable and therefore comfortable. Comforting. The signal of the end of a rant. "God, I could've just killed her."

Or him, as the case may be.

Or him.

Then the comeback, perfectly timed. Two beats, and the other would say, "But what would you do with the body?"

Only this time, no one laughed.

"Seriously, Honey," my dad began. "Amber told us about—"

"—what he did to Ashley," picked up my mom. "Unthinkable. Poor little—"

"—kid. Didn't deserve that. You need—"

"—the kids need. You need— "

"Judas Priest, even we need him out of your life."

"Soon."

"Okay." I said.

"What?" my dad said.

"I said, 'Okay.' Look, you might as well know, I've already asked him to move out. Several times. He just keeps getting weirder and weirder. And then when he…"

"Ashley."

"Right. That's why I went back to work. Because he won't be around much longer."

Then my mom started to tear up. And she turned to leave because, of course, in our family, private displays of emotion are as unacceptable as public ones.

"Okay, Honey," my dad said, following her to the door. "That's good. That's just fine. But if he—if you— if he tries anything—you know—funny, you call me. Then after an hour or so, the police. 'Cause I could just kill him."

They left without my requisite tag line, turning in tandem as they got to the steps and saying in unison, "We love you."

My dad added, "Honey."

At nearly midnight, Tim had still not returned, so I went to bed, expecting to fall asleep immediately. Blessing or curse, I have always had an ability to go to sleep quickly and then sleep deeply and soundly. Except for two nights a month. Back-to-back, every month, I'll go to sleep quickly as usual, but sleep only two or three hours. Then, for no apparent reason, I'll be wide awake, rested and refreshed, often full of an energy I cannot expend without making noise that may awaken my family. I've thought about charting these sleepless nights to see if there is a correlation between my cycles and the moon's, but invariably forget about them once they are over. This was to be the first of my two-a-month bad nights, but I didn't know it then. So I fell asleep, unconcerned about Tim's whereabouts or well-being. Drunk on his ass in some parking lot or scrumping some skank in the back seat of his car, I simply did not care. In the morning, I'd start packing his things. Enough was enough.

Was enough.

Was enough.

What an odd word 'enough' is. We should spell it eenuff, shouldn't we? I wonder where it came from.

Then suddenly I was awake. I was still alone in my bed, and the lights were still off, so I didn't immediately know whether or not Tim had returned. But I was fully awake, as usual on these nights, so I got up to fix myself a cup of honey tea, which never fails to comfort me. I puttered about the kitchen for a few minutes before a darker heap in the dark living room caught my attention. I switched on the nearest lamp and was not surprised to see Tim sprawled out on the sofa. At least he'd had the decency to keep out of the bedroom. The living room reeked of stale beer and regurgitation. I checked the floor for vomit, intending to make him clean it up himself. I was damned if I was going to do it. Bastard. What was even worse, a third stench drifted from him: urine. He'd pissed himself. On my freaking sofa, no less.

He was so profoundly passed out that he wasn't even snoring. Tim usually snored like it was an avocation. He even snored before he was asleep, as he was drifting off. He snored even if I rolled him over on his side, as I'd read about in a magazine article called "Sleeping With A Snorer." I could not believe I'd once found it comforting, snoring as auditory evidence of companionship. Shit. Now here he was, so disgustingly drunk that he'd pissed himself on my sofa.

My anger intensified with each heartbeat in my chest. Until this moment, I'd been disappointed, I'd been frightened, I'd been shocked and horrified, I'd been impatient and finally bored by this man. But I hadn't been truly angry. Now I was. He was in my house, in my life, mistreating my kids, burning my sheets, trashing my front yard, and now pissing on my sofa. I was sick to death of him. He was ugly and mean and quite possibly dangerous. It seemed to me that the dark heap in my living room, that sodden reeking mess, was not much more than garbage that needed to be hauled away. "Just kick him to the curb," I heard a voice in my head say. "Just take out the trash."

So I did.

We never used the front door. It was double-bolted so the kids would not be tempted to use it until the porch was finished. But I unbolted it and propped it open with a brick I'd decorated by painting on all twelve astrological symbols. A hot breeze blew into the room and warmed it, making Tim's offensive stench even more offensive. There was no screen or storm door yet; we'd planned on installing a new, more visually appealing and energy-efficient front door when the porch was done. Someday.

I did not think about what I was doing. I felt calm, detached, mechanical. I was aware of what I was doing, but was not thinking anything but 'Take out the trash,' 'Take out the trash,' 'Take out the trash.'

It was easy to roll him off the sofa onto the floor. Gravity did most of the work. Most shit does sink, said the voice. To the door, however, was another story. Which physical law could I use to drag him the last ten feet or so? True, he was tall, 6'1", he'd said, but then he was such a damned liar. Who knew how tall he really was? And who gave a reeking hot damn? His damp jeans made dragging even harder. Stupid bastard. The least he could have done was piss himself after I'd kicked him to the curb.

It was amazing, really, that even drunk he didn't wake up, didn't even moan. I've been drunk a few times in my life, drunk enough to pass out. But I don't think anyone could have dragged me to the curb without waking me up. So I pulled and pulled until I noticed that a corner of the area rug had gotten caught under the heel of his boot. And that reminded me of my seventh grade science class. Sure. Reduce the resistance. I rolled him completely onto the rug and began to drag that with him on it toward the front door. This helped tremendously. I was congratulating myself on that particularly useful retrieved memory and thinking about shit sinking and taking out the trash when a sudden movement in the boys' bedroom doorway clutched at my heart.

Ashley stood in the doorway with his eyes wide open. Oh God, I thought, he's seen me. What should I say? What could I say? I'd have to explain it all to him, explain Tim's drunkenness and his stench, and that I was just—just—taking out the trash? Tears welled up in my eyes as I thought of Ashley, of Tim kicking him that day, of the sordid circumstances my own decisions had placed him in. I wanted to go to my son, to hold and comfort him. To tell him everything would be all right. And then I noticed his eyes.

His beautiful deep brown eyes were open, yes, but they were not focused. Not on me, not on Tim at his feet. He was staring blankly into space and fumbling with the fly on his pajamas. Oh God. He was sleepwalking again. He'd done this numerous times. Once at my folks' house I caught him just as he was about to urinate into their clothes dryer. He was still sound asleep, but on some deep level he knew he had to pee. I dropped Tim's arms and started toward Ashley, to guide him around the corner into the bathroom when suddenly he flipped his little penis out of his jammies and peed right in Tim's face.

There was nothing I could do. It was over before I fully realized what Ashe was doing. He tucked himself back into his fly, turned around, and went back to bed.

For a minute, I just stood there, processing the incident. Now, as I tell you this, I suppose that was the moment that could have changed everything, the entire course of my life. I could have left Tim there near the front door; I could have gone back to bed and dealt with his sorry excuses and foul mood in the morning. I could have. Maybe should have. Certainly would have.

But I didn't.

There was now one more stench to add to the collection that was Tim, and I still wanted it gone. Take out the trash. Just take out the trash.

Now, kicking him to the curb is just a figure of speech as we didn't actually have a curb. But we did have a shoulder of the road where we wheeled out our refuse every Monday morning.

I figured that would be good enough. I figured he'd get the message if he woke up in that same spot, especially if his belongings were out there with him. And that's what I decided to do. After I'd dragged him to the road, I'd come back in and throw his shit together and drag it out there, too. I smiled at the thought. I'm sure I did.

The problem was that I was so focused on dragging him out the door that I forgot there was nothing on the other side of it. I'd forgotten about the pit. As I got right at the threshold, backing out as I dragged Tim, I almost lost my balance and toppled out the door myself. How could I have forgotten that half-finished eyesore?

I know what you are thinking: that I did not, either, forget it. That I'd planned it. That would be the case against me. I'd planned the whole thing. Premeditated. But I swear to you that I did not. The bed thing I did consider, well, fantasize about. Briefly. But that night, the night I'm telling you about, just happened. One thing just led to another. And then another.

So I was teetering there on the threshold with a dead-to-the-world stinking Tim on a rug. And I suddenly realized that I could not kick Tim to the curb. I could not get him over the open pit. I stood above him considering this for I don't know how long. I just stood there looking down on him, thinking nothing, feeling nothing, planning nothing—I swear to God.

Then, still thinking nothing, I stepped around him, to his feet, and shoved until his head was out the door. Then I lifted his feet, his legs that were so unbelievably heavy. But then my old pal gravity lent me her helping hand, and I reverse-somersaulted him out into the pit, area rug and all. That would just have to do. Let him wake up in the pit. Let him wake up and smell himself in the morning. Stupid bastard.

And I shut the door and bolted it and went about cleaning up my living room, stripping the upholstery fabric from the seat cushions and washing them (thank God for zippers). Then I went over the hardwood floor with some Murphy's Oil Soap which took care of the last lingering odors. Then I took a couple of contractor's bags and went through the house throwing into them everything that belonged to Tim or reminded me of him. Everything except my sewing machine and the double strand of cultured pearls he'd given me. I put the overstuffed bags neatly on the back porch.

Then I did something I hadn't done since I left the city: I locked the back door, too. It might have been wickedly comical to see him wake up and wonder where the hell he was and what the hell had happened, but he might not find it so amusing. If on any level he figured out that I'd had a hand in deciding his sleeping quarters, he might turn nasty. At least with a locked door, I'd have time to call for help if I needed it. The sky was lightening before I could catch a quick hot shower and go to bed.

In the morning, I called my folks. I told them Tim was moving out and I didn't want the kids around in case things got ugly. Could they go over there for awhile? Of course, the doting grandparents said yes, making me promise to call them if I needed anything. Anything. As I watched the three precious young people who'd given my life a center, a purpose, I had the same mixed feelings I always had on leaving them or they leaving me, for however short a time: a sickening feeling of loss and abandonment. A terrible fear that this good-bye might be our last. No matter how tired or discouraged or frustrated or angry I might feel, I tried always to make partings loving and positive, just in case.

Once they were out of sight, I set about the ugly task of getting rid of Tim. It was late morning, so he'd had plenty of time to sleep it off in the pit. It did not occur to me to dread this final confrontation. If he were not willing to go peacefully, I'd just put up my stoneface mask. I loaded the trash bags into his car, then went up front to the pit.

"Tim? Time to get up. Get up and get out," I said, peering over the side wall. For the most part, the area rug covered him up. Only part of his face and his left hand were visible. He hadn't moved in the slightest was what I noticed first. Then, fast on that impression was the grayish blue tint to his skin. And I knew, I just knew. It was more of a visceral understanding than a cognitive realization. Tim was dead. And I'd killed him. He must have hit his head on a chunk of the concrete rubble, although I could see no blood. The sight of blood would have shocked me into action, but as I saw none, I entered an oddly disconnected cold calm. I felt weak in the knees, which sounds like another cliché until you'd experienced it. I needed to sit down, so I did, on the bottom step near Jason's right handprint.

What was I going to do? Call the police, of course. Of course. That would have been the right thing to do. But I just couldn't. I kept seeing my kids walking away from me and what it would do to them to know for all the rest of their lives that their mother was a murderer. How would that twist their young psyches? How would they ever live it down? Would the courts let my parents keep them or would Scott claim them? Well, Amber and Ashley at least. And what would it do to them to be separated from their mother and their baby brother? And how could I survive even one day separated from them? If I could not tuck them into bed, read them a book or tell them a story? If I could never again hear them laugh or argue or call for me? If I could never again feel the moist warmth of my children's breath against my neck as we cuddled?

If I couldn't wipe their tears or runny noses or feel the solidity of their bodies as they leaned against my leg or shoulder? What if they ended up in foster care with strangers raising them? I'd had a friend in junior high who was in foster care; her foster "parents" treated her like an indentured servant and dressed her in rummage sale clothes, and not nice ones, either. What if that were my children's fate? It all seemed so damned unfair. I hadn't meant to kill him. I just wanted him gone, out of my life, and out of my house. Why should my kids be punished so severely for something that I did that I didn't mean to do?

And so I sat, these thoughts and images going around and around in my head. I had no defense to offer, no justifiable homicide plea. I killed him in his sleep. And even if he was a creep getting creepier all the time, he didn't deserve this. Poor schmuck. Poor creepy fucked-up schmuck. I pictured newspaper headlines and grainy photos of me in handcuffs being led off by police, my kids standing helplessly, forlornly by. And for what? I did not benefit from his death, and I did not revel in it, either. It was an accident, but who would ever believe that? I didn't think about myself, about the loss of my own freedom, about my own shame and social disgrace. I was, however, terrified for my kids.

I'm not sure how long I sat there, hours or minutes. Time has always had a slippery quality for me. "The other day" might mean anything from yesterday to last year. "In a minute" might be a few seconds to never, especially if something else captures my attention. So I don't know how much time passed between my getting up and starting to shovel rubble into the pit on top of Tim and my realizing what I was doing. It was as if I were on automatic pilot. And then, when I did realize what I'd started, I was appalled. Absolutely appalled. How could I have done such a thing? How could I calmly start to bury Tim as if he were a pet cat hit by a car?

But then the circular thinking started again. I thought about my defense that I hadn't planned to kill Tim, but now that he was covered in rubble, who would believe that? I thought about all the movies I'd seen and the books and stories I'd read, and how I'd sat there judging the characters and condemning the writers and criticizing the authenticity of the plot. Who would do that? I'd ask. Who in their right mind would act that way? And I felt so disconnected from myself that I could do the same with my own actions. Not realistic. Not defensible. Not logical. Not rational.

But real. It was real. I kept shoveling. And when the piles Tim had brought out were diminished, I brought up more in the rusty red wheelbarrow. I just kept working and working, still on automatic, until the rubble was level with the side walls. I hadn't eaten or drank or toileted myself. I had just worked and worked. And I was tired, bone tired, but I could not stop. I knew about smell. Tim would be starting to smell. Soon. And the smell would trigger questions; my kids would notice and ask too many questions.

Tim had insisted on explaining everything he did, every step of every chore he took on. Mixing concrete was one of the one-on-one tutorials he'd conducted. And, although he was at his most boring during these tedious attempts to impart knowledge, I'd listened. I'd watched, and I'd listened, and I'd helped. I knew how to secure the supports for the third wall of the cap, and I knew the right mix of cement, water, and the sandy gravel Tim had insisted was better than the pre-mix I'd suggested. I knew to mix the three together to the consistency of cake batter. I didn't know how to cut re-bar although I'd watched Tim do this, too. So I'd have to do without the reinforcement. Maybe it was less important for the tops of things than for the bottoms. He hadn't said anything about having to use re-bar for the cap. But I remembered his debating between a four or a six-inch cap. Now that the job was mine, and considering its primary purpose, I would have liked a foot-thick slab.

Knowing how to do something is not the same as doing it. I'd learned that. It takes a matter of seconds to think through how to accomplish a thing, but the physical reality is always something else. This task was a nightmare. First, I tried to use the mudbox Tim had brought home, but it was too much for me. And it seemed illogical to mix the concrete in the box and then load it into the wheelbarrow. So I started mixing the concrete right in the wheelbarrow and not mixing it as thoroughly as Tim would have insisted on. Then I'd wheel it up the makeshift ramp he'd set up, teetering dangerously but losing only half of one load when I lost my balance. To give the dead guy his due, he'd perfectly calculated the needed quantities of cement and gravel. There was nearly none left by the time I finished. The sun was well on its way to the horizon and I was shaking uncontrollably, physically pushed to my absolute limit, as I did a half-assed job of leveling and smoothing the top. Tim would not have approved. Tomorrow, I estimated, it would have set up enough to break down the supports. It was a far from perfect job, but it was done. I went inside and drank probably a gallon of water in huge gulps. Sweaty and filthy and blowing cement dust from my nostrils, I headed for the shower when the phone rang.

"Mom?" Amber's voice warmed the chill along my spine I'd felt all day despite the heat.

"Mom? Can we sleep over? Pleeeeeese? We're watching really, really old Mickey Mouse cartoons that Puppa bought and they're not over yet. Pleeeeeese? PleasePleasePleasePleasePlease?"

And I laughed. God help me, I laughed. After the unpleasantness of the night, the horror of the day, the backbreaking and macabre job I'd just completed, I laughed. Amber could always make me laugh. And, as she well knew, a quintuple Please always worked.

"Mom? Puppa wants to talk to you. I love you, okay?" Amber said. I could hear the boys squabbling in the background, calling Amber a brat because they wanted to talk to me, too. And then squabbling with each other for the simple joy of squabbling. I could hear my mom defuse them with the promise of blueberry pancakes for breakfast, then my dad was on the line.

"Honey? Are you all right? Is everything all right? We thought maybe you'd call."

"I'm sorry, Daddy. It's just turned out to be—" I looked down at the clothes I planned to throw away rather than wash, "—to be a lot—messier than I'd expected."

"Is there anything you need? Is he gone?"

Suddenly, all my repressed emotions of the day began to rise in me like the feeling just before you throw up and I was afraid I was going to start laughing again, but a different laugh than Amber evoked.

"Gone. Yup. All gone. Gone bye-bye."

"Honey? Are you all right? Should we come over?"

Good grief no. Hell no. Good God no. Zeus and zucchini no.

"No!" I must have shouted. Struggled for control. "No, Daddy, no. But thank you."

"Are you positive? You sound kind of—"

"No. I mean yes. I mean no. Yes, I'm positive. No, I don't think you need to come over. But thank you. Thank you, Daddy." And then I was struggling to keep from breaking down in tears, from confessing everything, from begging for help, begging for forgiveness.

"Well, all right then. If you're sure. Your mother says to come over for blueberry pancakes in the morning. About eight."

"Will do. About eight." I knew this was her way of making sure I'd be there by eight-thirty.

"Honey? Are you sure—"

"Yeah, Daddy, I'm sure. I'm fine. Gonna take a shower, go to bed."

He must have heard something in my voice. But he let me off. Actually, I was relieved. By the questions he asked, I knew he hadn't gone anywhere, hadn't seen me working on the porch. I wouldn't have to explain about that, at least.

I showered until the hot water ran out and fell into bed, my bed, diagonally. A luxury known only by the single. As expected, I fell instantly into the deep, imageless sleep of the completely exhausted, but then woke with a sudden realization: Tim's car.

It was still in the driveway. Shit. If he left today, then how did he leave? On foot? Shit, shit, shit. I ran to the door, to the key rack he'd made to try to get me organized. It drove him nuts that I could never find my keys. It was maybe twenty-five feet from the bed to the key rack at the back door, but that short distance was far enough for me to clearly visualize an empty hook where his key should have been, to imagine his keys safely tucked into the left front pocket of his jeans. The jeans he was wearing last night. The jeans he was wearing when I buried him. I had reached nearly total panic by the time I'd made that short sprint. I was so convinced I'd buried his car keys along with him that I could not, at first, completely accept that his keys hung right where he put them. Unfailing creature of habit was our Tim.

As I went to pull his car into the garage, a place it had never been before, I noticed the trash bags of his belongings. For sure he would not be needing anything from those bags, so I piled them up with everything else that I would haul out to the road for Monday morning. Then I pulled his car inside the garage and slid shut the garage door. For good measure, I threw the latch, but had no padlock to secure it. Later, I'd figure out what to do with his car. Tomorrow, I thought, or the next day. Soon. I went back to bed and back to sleep.

God help me, I slept like the proverbial baby.

What if you disappeared from the face of the earth and no one even noticed? What if you'd lived 34 years and no one cared if you lived another? Impossible?

Improbable? Unlikely?

I agree. Yet, true. Unbelievably, unthinkably true. For the first week or so, I jumped when the phone rang, hesitated to answer it. I expected the shop to call, concerned about his absence. I expected someone, some friend or lover or co-worker to call or stop by to see what was wrong. I even half-expected the police to show up at my door, handcuffs at the ready. What I did not expect was nothing. Silence. No questions, no inquiries, no accusations. I'd prepared a variety of fabrications and practiced them in my head, rejecting and revising as I went.

Finally, I decided that ignorance would be the most believable response. I had no idea where he went. He'd left no forwarding address. Maybe one of the women he was seeing? Who knew? I'd been blessed, or cursed, with a baby face that was irritating most of the time, like when I continued to be carded years after my 21st birthday, but that came in handy if I were denying some culpability or other. I could make my pale blue eyes seem bland and blank by unfocusing them slightly. I could lie my teeth out, and people always believed me. They would again, I convinced myself. The trick would be not to over-do the details. If I didn't know much, I couldn't betray much. He'd not come home that night, that's all. I'd seen it coming. I'd found a woman's phone number in his shirt pocket, but had thrown it away and didn't remember her name. A Saginaw number, I'd thought, but couldn't remember any of it. Sorry.

I went to work and took care of the kids and the house. I cooked and did laundry and dishes. I spent time with my folks, helping my dad weed his vegetable garden, helping my mom can tomatoes. And I waited. And waited. Then I waited some more. But for nothing. No one. Not even his work. It was as if he'd never been. After a few months, late into fall, I began to relax. True, I never even glanced at the front porch. What I mean is that I studiously avoided looking at it, the way we learn to avoid looking at cemeteries or funeral processions or homeless people. As if, if we don't look at them, really look at them, they won't exist, won't need or want anything from us, won't remind us of what might have been, might yet, or what most certainly will be. Coming home or leaving, I avoided looking at the porch. We'd planned some minor landscaping, a couple of transplanted spirea bushes, a few daylilies, but I could never get myself to go that close. The new drain field had torn up the scrubby grass that had been there and we'd never re-seeded. So there was not much grass to cut. Besides, my dad had taken on that chore. He insisted that with his ride-on mower it was not a big deal. He assured me that he welcomed any excuse to be outside, anyway. And I knew this was true.

If you are expecting me to tell you about ghostly appearances, cold spots, or eerie noises, you will be disappointed. There was no "Telltale Heart" beating in my conscience. No night terrors. Tim was as unobtrusive in death as he had been before we moved to Lincoln Road.

I slept as peacefully and predictably as ever. But before you judge me harshly, let me confess that my lack of feelings of guilt puzzled me, too. I have always been an extremely conscientious and tender-hearted person. To a fault, perhaps. But I felt nothing, felt as detached from what I'd done as if it were the last half of a news story I'd heard on TV. As if it were something done by someone far away that I didn't know. And this did puzzle me. When I allowed myself to think of it, that is. Mostly, I did not.

At first, I focused with all my might on whatever I had to do next: another load of laundry, another story read to the kids, another meal to prepare and then to clean up after. And I went to work. Without realizing it, I made myself more and more available to take on an extra day if someone didn't show or called in sick. By the time I'd driven as little as a quarter of a mile out of my driveway, I detached entirely from what I'd done. At work, it was even easier to focus on what had to be done next. What had to be done next was clear-cut and simple: schlep drinks, clear tables, empty or replace ashtrays, sop up spills, smart-ass with customers, fend off advances. At the end of the night, I'd dump my tip glass into my purse without counting it. Then I'd drive home, staying focused on the road ahead, the day ahead. However, I never planned beyond the day, expecting at any moment for it to be my last day of freedom.

Deep inside me, in the darkest, stillest corner where I steadfastly refused to go, I knew that I would have to pay, and pay dearly, for what I'd done. Murder will out, you know. A dire admonition with deep roots in truth: Murder will out. The best I could hope for was to stall my fate. Just one more day. Just one more after that. Then one more.

And I was so busy focusing that I'd completely forgotten about Tim's damned car. I'd shut the garage door and then forgotten it. An inappropriate bit of humor occurred to me: I'd discovered what to do with the body, but the damned car stumped me. When I remembered, I began to try to figure out a solution, but every solution had a "but" attached, a great big hairy pimpled "but."

If I drove it to the shop parking lot to abandon it there, how would I get home? Who could I ask to become an unwitting accomplice after the fact? The same with the airport, although that made no sense. Tim had proudly told me he'd never left the state of Michigan and had no desire to, by any means of transportation. And it made no sense either when I considered my supposed supposition that he'd moved in with some girlfriend, just as he'd used me to move out on his wife. If, in fact, that is what happened. I even considered dropping the car off downtown with the keys inside. It would be stripped and torched before I could get home. But how would I get home? If we still lived in town, I could walk. But out here in the boonies?

Hitchhike? Right. I'd done this when I was young and stupid. Very young and very stupid. But then, when all this blew up, as it was sure to, there was the risk of some good Samaritan who'd given me the lift doing the decent thing and testifying against me. And again, who could I ask to drive me home after I'd dropped it off somewhere?

My dad would. My old friend Becky might. Two people in the world to trust. My dad because, for all his faults and the mistakes he made in raising us, he was my dad. He would accept any excuse I gave, but his instincts are as sharp as mine, and he'd know. And it would, ultimately, cost him. It would implicate him. Becky might, too. Becky and I had been friends since the year I'd graduated from high school. We knew many of each other's darkest secrets, but none were as dark as this. And again, I could not implicate my friend. I thought of one absurd solution after another, then discarded it.

I could take the damned car to CashForCars, but then again, how to get home again? Amber had been exploring the deepest boundary of our property and had discovered an old rusted-out car in the woods. I had forbidden her to play back there, warning of the dangers of tetanus from rusty metal cuts. But I did consider driving Tim's car through the back field and abandoning it.

Now, I think that might have been the best solution; but at the time I thought that, should Amber's curiosity override my warning, she'd find the second car, certainly recognize it, and ask awkward questions I would not know how to answer.

I thought about leaving the car in the garage, selling the house, and moving away. But again, how to explain the contradicting stories? I'd planned to swear Tim simply left. No one would believe he'd left on foot, and it was too late for me to report him missing.

The most ridiculous solution was inspired by Tim's own garden: I could dig a huge hole, big enough for a small swimming pool, and bury the sucker. But even I could see the impossibility of such an undertaking. Me and a shovel?

Oh, yes. The final solution presented itself.

My folks were going to Chicago on a long weekend with a group of their community theatre friends. I'd arranged to take the weekend off as I had no other babysitter I trusted enough with my kids but knew I'd miss the money. Money is always an issue for a single mom. So money was foremost in my mind as we planned for a picnic in the "way back" of our property, as the kids called it. We could stay on our own land but get away from routine at the same time. The picnic turned into a camping trip when we decided to borrow my dad's pop-up camper and sleep out.

Because my folks built their house deeply back from the road and our house was right up at the road, it was more convenient to use their bathroom and kitchen for our campout. I wasn't as enthusiastic about camping out, but figured that if that year's incredible Indian Summer collapsed around us, we could still camp out— just on my folk's living room floor. So I agreed to try it.

Of course, as always happens with any excursion, near or far, we forgot things. So I made several trips back to our house, leaving Amber to watch the boys for a few minutes at a time. I was simply trying to enjoy our time together, but kept thinking about the money I was not making that weekend when, on my last trip to the house, I thought about the car. It was worth something.

Resenting the interest he had to pay on the loan, Tim had paid it off early, working an obscenely small amount of overtime to do so. So I wouldn't be doing anything much more illegal than signing his name on the title and the back of the registration. I made a For Sale sign with a piece of poster board and a purple crayon, drove the car up to the road, and added the instruction to honk if interested. I wasn't thinking about the neighbors, or the cops, or any possible acquaintance of Tim's happening by. I was, stupidly, I now realize, focused only on the allure of more money.

I know what you are thinking. Yes, I knew it was wrong. Of course I knew that. And unlikely, too. I've already told you how little traveled Lincoln Road was. Why on earth I thought someone would just happen to be driving by with a pocketful of cash and a need for a '75 Dodge Charger is beyond me. But we'd been lucky with the porch wood, after all. Anything could happen. So for a day and a half Tim and his car were a mere 25 feet from each other, but the car was out in the open, and he was all nicely covered up.

On the second day of our adventure in the Way Back, which the kids were really getting into but which left me stiff and cranky (I'm just not the roughing-it type), I heard a car horn coming from the house. At first I was confused. Who the hell could that be? But then I remembered. I asked Amber to watch the boys as I hurried to the house. My stupidity was foremost in my mind. What the hell had I been thinking? The fit would surely hit the shan now. This was bound to be the police who recognized the car from a description of some missing person report filed by God knows whom. Shit,

shit, shit. What was I thinking? No amount of money was worth this risk. I swore at myself and to myself. If I skated out of this one by some miracle, I'd put the car back in the garage, spray paint the garage windows so no one could look in, padlock the damned door shut and get the hell out of there with my kids as fast as we could possibly go. We would not look back. We would not pass Go. We would not collect $2,000.

By the time it occurred to me that if I didn't respond to the horn honking whoever it was would just go away and I could still save my ass, it was too late. The driver of the blue and white Chevy van had seen me, waved, and started in my direction. At least it wasn't a cop.

At least, not an on-duty one.

"Hey there," the florid middle-aged man said, holding out his hand as he approached. "How you doin'? I'm interested in your car. That your bottom line?"

I'd asked for $2,300, hoping for $2,000 and giving myself some bargaining room.

"It isn't mine," I said, telling the truth. "I'm selling it for my brother," I added, lying. "He's in the Army, in Germany."

"No shit," he said, reddening even more. "I mean, no kidding. Sorry, Ma'm."

"I've heard worse," I assured him, not wanting to lose the sale.

"I just meant I was in the Army in Germany, too. Where is he?"

"Where were you?" Slick, see? I can be very, very slick. All most people really want is a tenth of one percent of a chance to talk about themselves, and they always give themselves away about the topic. All anyone else has to do is listen. And I listened.

I listened as this idiot chattered away about things that happened thirty or more years ago that no one gives a crap about anymore and probably didn't give a crap about when it happened. I listened and nodded and Oh Really-ed and When was that-ed as he looked over the car. Under the hood, in the trunk, kicked the tires, the whole unnecessary ball of wax. Then he sat behind the wheel and inhaled.

"Smoker, eh?"

"Pardon?"

"Your brother. He a smoker? Car reeks."

Shit. Shit. Shit. Shit. Shit.

"Yeah, like a fiend. Sorry." There went my chance to kill two birds with one car sale.

"Don't be," he said with an expansive smile that revealed a gap where one of his eyeteeth was missing. "Me, too. Nasty, nasty habit," he said with a chuckle. "This'll keep the old lady from borrowing my car."

He started the engine, revved it entirely too much for any practical purpose, then agreed to full price if he could come get it in the morning. He pulled a wad of bills out of his pants pocket and peeled off hundreds as if they were toilet paper. He tucked the rest back into his pocket and handed the key back to me.

"No, no. It's yours now. You come back for it any time you want. I may not be home. You know, church tomorrow," I lied. "The title's in the glove compartment. He's already signed off it."

"Well, well, now, he just thought of everything, didn't he?" the guy said, his eyes narrowing.

All my alarms went off. How would I know if this were an undercover cop, or a buddy of Tim's? I'd never met anyone he knew. One day at the mall, we'd seen someone he said he worked with, but Tim had ducked behind a rack of overalls to avoid having to speak to him. Worse, what if this were his alleged brother?

I was having a hard time maintaining my veneer of calm innocence when the guy spoke again.

He reached into his shirt pocket—I was sure it would be for a badge—and pulled out a wadded up package of unfiltered cigarettes. "You a pretty little thing. You live alone way out here? Don't that make you nervous?"

No, you nasty old fuck, I live with a virtual arsenal of weapons I am well trained to use, I wanted to say. But I still wanted that car out of here, and I wanted to keep that money. So instead, I smiled sweetly and told him, "Oh no. I don't live here at all. This is our dad's house. Maybe you know him? Police Chief Mayfield?"

That did it. Now, I just might have been in some deep steaming caca if this guy were from around here, but I hadn't yet met anyone who was from around here. Everyone seemed always to be just passing through. Or just moved out here from the city, trying to move away from the rising crime.

"Nope, nope," the guy said, straightening up his posture and his attitude. "Just happened to be taking a short cut home. Saw your car—your brother's car. Thought I'd stop." He muttered some other quasi-amenities as he hauled his fat ass back into his van. "I'll be back in the morning. Old lady'll bring me."

As if I gave half a shit. He could strap the sucker on his back and slither off with it for all I gave a crap. But I smiled sweetly. "Whatever works for you folks," I said. "My brother thanks you."

He drove off as I started back to the kids. I don't even know any damned police chief, much less know if there's any Mayfields around here. Where the hell had that name even come from? Shit, I should have used Tim's last name for our imaginary shared dad. The name should have matched the title. Oh well. I smiled as I walked through the weed-choked garden Tim had worked so hard to plant. I smiled as I fingered those hundreds in my pocket. One more day, I thought, just one more day.

But the guy didn't wait that long. When I came back to the house a few hours later for another jar of peanut butter, the damned car was gone. I wished the guy a generous helping of lung cancer and breathed a sigh of relief. I used a couple hundred dollars to outfit the kids for back-to-school. With the rest, I paid off my own car. One less monthly payment to worry about. Back then, I wasn't yet savvy enough to calculate how much interest I saved. I was very present-oriented.

But this part of my story isn't over yet. In order for you to judge me fairly, you need to know all of it. Everything. Three more things happened before autumn ended. None of them were things I could have predicted. One of them I am deeply ashamed of, even more so than the business with Tim, which is how I started to think of it: The Business With Tim. Not the murder, not Tim's death; not Tim's leaving. But The Business With Tim, capped like that, like the title of a story. The Business With Tim taught me much about myself, so you can see the experience was not without its redeeming value. It was tremendously educational. Without it, I may not ever have learned just how far I would be able to go to protect my kids. And myself. And if someone would have tried to tell me what I was capable of, I would have been shocked and deeply offended. I would never have been able to believe it.

But I'll tell you the other thing first. It is easier to tell because it is less painful.

When I pay close attention to my instincts, when I take the advice of my intuition, I seldom regret it. When I don't, I always regret it. My impulse to sell Tim's car when I did might seem rash; after all, it was doing no harm in the garage. But the coincidence of my parents being out of state (which rarely happened) at the very same time I was frantically trying to think of a solution seemed so fortuitous as to border on the divinely ordained. Plus, the money really helped. So I was grateful. But I was even more grateful just a couple weeks later when a man I'd never seen before showed up at my door.

And this time, it was about Tim.

When I responded to his knock, I got a creepy feeling. Like a chill, although our Indian Summer was holding on way past predictions. And I got this chill before I got a good look at him. About Tim's height, but heavier and with lighter hair and eyes, he resembled Tim only slightly. Until he spoke.

In a voice exactly like Tim's he said, "Hello. You don't know me, but my name is Steve. Steve Whittacre. I may not have the right place, but my brother gave me this address." He offered a scrap of paper as evidence. "I'm sorry to bother you, but he said he lived here. He said he'd bought a place out here."

"Liar." The word escaped my mouth before I had time to adjust my attitude.

Steve didn't react at all. He just stood there, still on the back porch. In the country, thank God, people just naturally come to the back door. If someone shows up at the front door, you can be assured of two things: one, they are strangers; two, it is bad news. In this case, it would have been horrifying. Steve would have been standing on his brother's grave.

"He lied," I repeated. "This is my house. I own this house."

And then I caught myself, tried to back pedal. "But he did live here. Did. He moved out. Quite a while now."

"I see," said Steve, still not seeming surprised. "Well, my point is, he borrowed my mud box a while ago and never returned it. I asked him to bring it back, but he didn't."

"I don't know where he went. He just left."

"Yup. But I see it's out there by the garage."

"He didn't leave a forwarding address or phone number. Nothing."

"So, if you don't mind, I'll just load it up and take it home."

"I don't know how you can get ahold of him."

"That's all right. I just came for my mud box."

He started to move away from the door when I realized I'd been answering questions he hadn't asked. Stupid. Why not just blurt out, "I killed the son-of-a-bitch"? Stupid.

"Wait," I said, stepping outside. "I'll help. I'm sorry. I didn't mean to be rude. I was just surprised. At first I thought—"

"That I was Timmy? A lot of people say we look alike. I've never seen it, myself. We aren't much alike. I'm sorry I startled you. I would have called, but he didn't give me a number. Just the address. Said he didn't have a phone."

"Another lie," I said under my breath. But Steve heard.

"That's what he does best. Lie. That and—I hope he didn't hurt you."

"Hurt me?"

We'd been strolling over to the mud box as we talked. Steve pulled the box away from the weeds that had ensnared it and tipped it right side up.

"Shit," he muttered. "Stupid bastard. I told Damn it."

"I'm sorry?"

"Tim. I told him to make sure he cleaned it out good. I didn't even want to lend it to him, but—you know—he is my brother."

I'd done the best I could when I sprayed it out after

The Business With Tim, but I could see now how much concrete I'd missed.

"I'm sorry," I said, in all sincerity.

Steve seemed like a truly nice person. But then, so had Tim when I first met him. Clearly my judgment of men could not be trusted.

"Don't be," Steve assured me. "It wasn't your fault."

Obviously, he didn't need my help loading up his truck, so I watched and we talked a little more.

"You asked if Tim had hurt me. What did you mean?"

"No, I don't guess he'd've told you about any of that, would he?"

I just waited. I wanted to hear whatever he had to say.

"Did he tell you about Debra? About his wife?"

I nodded. Of course. Little old homewrecker me.

"Did he tell you—oh hell, you might as well know—he used to come home drunk. He's been drinking too much since he was 15 or so. He can be nasty, real nasty. With or without the booze. One minute he's all aw-shucks-ma'm and the next he's just hardscrabble mean."

I nodded. I'd seen this.

"Well, the more he drinks, the more the nasty comes out. He used to come home drunk and beat the shit out of his wife."

Steve paused here and I could see the muscles in his jaw twitching just as Tim's had when he was angry. He looked at me and shook his head. "Only a coward hits a woman. I told him that, too. When I found out what he was doing I told him I didn't want him around until he got his act together. Cut him off. Then I don't see him for two, three years when he shows up to borrow my mud box. But my wife's sister knows his wife, so we heard all about it. I guess it was that same day—or the next. Timmy tied one on and went home to smack Debra around some more. I guess she took it, or seemed to, until he passed out. Then she took a cast iron skillet and showed him the backside of it. While he slept."

Most shocking to me was Steve's tone. We were talking about his brother, but he seemed to relish telling this story.

"You didn't—you don't like him, do you?" I asked.

"Like him? Like him? He's my brother, you know. I should feel some kind of brotherly love for him, even when I don't approve of his actions. But I don't. There's always been something just wrong about him. Born wrong or something. We had a springer spaniel puppy once. Sweet, fat little thing. But it was born wrong, too. Go into a rage at the drop of a hat. First few times, I thought it was funny. I didn't get it. Sweet little puppy snapping and snarling at anything in its way. Drew blood on my wife one night. It wasn't funny anymore. Vet explained it, said it was 'springer rage.' Said it'd only get worse. Recommended we put her down."

There were tears in his eyes that he brushed away with his shirt sleeve. "Hardest thing I've ever had to do. Hold that sweet little thing while the vet put her down. Damned shame."

He didn't need to explain the analogy; I got it.

"I'm sorry."

"'S all right. Been awhile, but I can't seem to get over it. You'd think by now—"

Then he looked at me, really looked at me, before he said, "So, did he?"

"Hurt me? No. But I sensed he wanted to. He hurt my boy, though."

"Bastard."

"That's what I said. I kicked him out and haven't heard from him since."

"Don't expect you will. He's done this before, too. Mom and Dad haven't heard from him in maybe seven years. Not one phone call, not one card or letter. Nothing."

"Your parents? He told me they were dead."

"Bastard." Steve climbed into his truck and shut the door.

"Before you go—there are other things he said. Now I'm wondering. I don't know what else he lied about."

"Probably everything, but go ahead. Ask."

"Debra? He said she was stalling the divorce. He said he didn't know if she'd ever let go completely."

"Lie. Final six months flat from the cast iron skillet. Kicked him out and never looked back."

"Their child? Was it a boy or a girl?"

"Would've been a boy, the doctor said. If he hadn't beat it out of her."

"Bastard."

Steve nodded. "Anything else?"

"Maybe. He said he was part Indian."

"That's true. Quarter Cherokee through our dad's side."

"He said he was descended from John Muir."

"Lie. John Myer, maybe. Dirt farmer on our mom's side. Nobody famous or even interesting. Just hard working stiffs like us."

"He said he had a heart condition. But I didn't believe it. He didn't act like a person who could die at any moment."

"Well, now, that's the irony, ain't it? That happens to be the truth. He was born with a faulty valve, and the world'd be a better place if he did pop off. Just too mean to die, I guess."

He must have seen something on my face; my mask must have slipped, because he said, "God, I'm sorry. That must've sounded terrible. I didn't mean it. Not really. He is my brother, after all. Are you all right?"

I had to force myself to speak. But first I had to think of something to say.

For the first time since that night, I was overcome with an impulse that I would come to know intimately: the impulse to confess. I desperately wanted to tell Steve about what I'd done. I suddenly wanted to unburden when I hadn't—until that moment—even been aware of being burdened.

Steve's voice sounded far away, as if he were speaking through an exceptionally bad connection.

"Are you all right?" he asked again. I heard the click of his truck door latch as he prepared to step back out into the driveway.

"No! Wait. I just remembered something," I said, turning back to the house.

On that night when I'd cleared the house of Tim's

possessions, I'd missed two things he'd tucked far back into the top shelf of the coat closet. I took them out to Steve.

"He forgot these," I said, handing over Tim's 35 mm camera and his binoculars in their crude leather cases he'd made himself.

"When you see him, will you give these to him?"

"If I see him, you mean," he said, accepting them through the window. "Are you sure you don't want to keep them? Might be able to get a couple hundred for 'em."

"No. No, that wouldn't be right. And I don't want any—"

"Reminders? Don't blame you. Sorry to bother you today. Dredge up all this. But it was good to meet you."

"Yes, me too. I mean, nice to meet you, too. And—Steve—thanks."

"For what?"

"The truth."

He just nodded, much as Tim might have, the good Tim anyway, and drove away. And I stood there staring at nothing while the dust settled.

I know what you're thinking. You're thinking, tough luck offing a guy who was gonna die anyway. And I guess you'd be right. As far as luck goes, I have the damnedest. I try and try and work and work, and I get shit on. Then I do something impulsive and unconscionable and stupid, and the most amazing things happen.

Once I entered a drawing for a new roof a hundred

times. One hundred 3x5 hand-lettered entries in one hundred hand-addressed envelopes with one hundred stamps. But I didn't win. The next winter an ice storm destroyed my roof, so my homeowner's policy covered not only the new roof, but new carpet and a new vinyl floor in the kitchen to boot.

Ten or eleven days after Steve's enlightening visit, Tim got mail. This in itself was a rarity. On retrospection, I realize his secretiveness was pathological. At the time, it irritated me, partly because incoming mail is an excellent way to keep tabs on someone. But Tim didn't even get junk mail. Everything was in my name except his car. Maybe he had a post office box; this would not surprise me. And of course, given the turn my own life was taking, I have little room to criticize. I guess you could say he taught me a thing or two, things I would need to know to live a strictly private life.

At any rate, it was a bit of a shock to see his name on an envelope in my mailbox.

Enough of a shock that my reflex was to toss it in the trash. But then I got the tingle. I get a tingle, even now, when a financial opportunity is presenting itself. I may still opt out of the opportunity, but at least I don't miss many out of lack of recognition. The envelope was smaller than a standard business envelope but larger than a letter size, and it had a window. There were only two things it could be: a bill or a check. The tingle said the latter, so I fished it out of the trash and tore it open. It was a check. A check for $18,500 from the Bureau of Indian Affairs. The accompanying letter said they had completed the verification of his claim, and this was his settlement. What claim? Tim had not said anything about making a claim, had dismissed it when I suggested it after watching some news segment. His dismissal I interpreted as meaning his claim to Native American heritage was a lie. But he must have begun the process without my knowledge. Probably meant to use the money to walk away from me. Not that he'd brought any such chunk of change into my house. I wondered if Steve knew about this and thought for a brief moment of tracking him down, urging him to apply, too.

Surely he and his wife could use 20 grand.

But then, of course, my newly-acquired sense of self-preservation kicked in. I'd have to confess that I'd received Tim's mail and, even more difficult to explain, had opened it. The old me, the scrupulous and highly-principled me, would never have opened anyone else's mail. Checked out the return address, maybe. Maybe held it up to the light. Maybe glanced at it once it was open and if it were left laying around. But never opened anyone else's mail. That was just despicable.

That word keeps occurring to me. Despicable. I would never have identified myself as despicable. But since I've started this confession, I realize that I have done many things in my life that I am not proud of. I have wronged many people, some by sins of commission, by things I did either deliberately or accidentally, some by sins of omission, by things I should have done but neglected to for whatever reason. I realize that now. But none of those bad things, nothing I did before The Business

With Tim was as horrific, as potentially life-altering. No, let me amend that, nothing was as life-altering. For my life altered; I have altered, irrevocably. Nothing I have done since would have been done, and certainly not done in the same way, if Tim's death hadn't happened. If I hadn't killed him. That one event on that one night altered the course of my life and the shame of it all is that I did not mean to do it. In my deepest heart, I don't think I would have cared much if he had died of natural causes or a drunk driving accident or a crime of passion committed by the jealous lover or husband of one of the women he was doing on the side. But I swear to you that I did not mean to kill him. I can't say as much for Sam, but that's another part of this story, the part I will get to eventually, the part that makes this confession so necessary.

So, how many people do you know who have been murdered? Besides Tim, I know three. Personally. Isn't that bizarre? I think it is a reflection of our violent times that I know this many. The first was a boy I knew in the ninth grade. He was blessed (or cursed) with exceptional good looks, like a young Troy Donahue if you know who he is. Tall, blonde, muscular. He didn't look like the fifteen-year old boy he was; he looked like a man all grown up and sexy and unaware of the potential consequences of messing around with the wrong married woman. They found his sexually mutilated body at the river's edge, and no arrest was ever made. The second person was a young woman who used to come in the first bar I worked in.

Katherine wasn't the bar type, and it showed. She wasn't particularly pretty or hip to the ways of the world, but she was sweet. Accommodating and gentle. She had a little kid from her first marriage that she was recently out of. I'd heard whispers that her first husband had beaten her, but I never asked her. We'd gotten to be casual friends, so I was glad when I heard she was seeing Pete, a bartender from a nearby bar whom I'd flirted with, too. Well, everyone had. Even the men. He was gorgeous and seemed like such a nice guy. They married, too quickly, I thought, but it wasn't any of my business. Then, a few months later, there was a fire at their place. Their gas line ruptured or something. She and her son were killed, and we all felt so bad for him. But the police were suspicious. I don't know why. We were all shocked when Pete was arrested for hiring someone to set the fire so he could get her life insurance. We didn't believe it. Not for a minute. Not Pete, everybody's best friend, everybody's big brother. But he confessed. He did time too, but not nearly enough. Several years later I walked into a sporting goods store and there he was, waiting on a customer. I thought I was going to throw up and ran out of the store. The third person was Scott's second ex-wife, Sydney.

My kids loved her and were sad when Scott and she divorced. A friend of hers told her that Alaska was the new land of opportunity, with men outnumbering women three to one. So Syd moved there and quickly met someone. But that someone had an ex-girlfriend who wanted him back in the worst way. So she hired someone to kill Sydney. When Scott called to ask me to tell the kids about her death, he told me the police in Alaska had to send for her dental records in order to make a positive identification. Of course, I left out that part when I told the kids. Dead is bad enough; murdered is worse. But dismembered is unthinkable, beyond horrific, and I didn't want them to envision this even in their worst nightmares.

But Sydney's death was still in the future when Tim got that check. And as you know, he had no real use for it. I reasoned that forgery and grand theft were minor charges compared to murder. Besides, if the check did not get cashed, someone might follow up on it, might trace it to me. It had come to my house, so even the most superficial investigation was clearly a threat. So I signed his name with a close approximation to the illegible scrawl he used. Then with a different color ink I signed my own beneath it, printing Deposit Only beneath that for weighty touch. Just cashing it might have prompted some questions, maybe even challenges, at the bank. But I figured depositing it would attract no attention. And it didn't. The cashier at the drive-through didn't bat an eyelash. I waited a full month before I wrote the first and only check against it: I paid off the house. Another monthly payment off my back.

Now, you need to remember this was a while ago. Real estate prices have soared since then, but I am still able to find incredible bargains. Yet, before I get to that, to how I've made my living and supported my kids, I need to confess that third despicable thing I did that autumn, the thing, in fact, that I most deeply regret to this very day. I am so ashamed of this single act that I have never told anyone. Ever. You are the first. And the last. I will never admit this again, and I have been trying to achieve redemption ever since. People have thought I am crazy for many reasons, not the least of which is my willingness to adopt abandoned dogs. At one point, I had six. Occasionally, someone asks why I have so many dogs. I've told them I love dogs because I've known so many humans. I've told them that dogs are the only source of unconditional love available to humans. But I've never told them about Libby.

At about the same time as receiving that financial boost, Amber was at a friend's house a mile or so away. When I went to pick up my daughter, there was a huge dog in their yard. As I stepped out of the car, this dog came bounding up to me and jumped. Picture a black lab the size of a Great Dane. When she jumped up on me with her paws squarely on my shoulders (which I barely felt, she'd landed so softly), she was taller than I. She bowed her head and licked my face in apparent delight.

Amber's friend's mom came out and said, "Oh, good, you've come. Your dog has been here all day. She's a sweetie, but I know she wants to go home."

I looked at Amber, who was very busy not looking at me, and said, "She's not mine. I've never seen her before." But the dog was so happy to see me that the woman didn't believe me.

"But she must be yours. Look at her."

The dog was all over me, wagging her tail, licking me and grinning. She took my hand in her huge soft mouth and led me to my car.

"If she's not yours," said the woman, "she ought to be."

"I agree," I said, "We'll take her home."

"Good. My husband was going to call the pound."

Which I could not allow. She took up the entire back seat, grinning all the way home. I'd never seen anything like her. And I fell in love. Instantly.

For two days, we were inseparable. If I took a step to the right, she was there. If I opened the refrigerator, she was looking over my shoulder. She slept in my bed, taking up half of it. Tim's half. I named her Libby. I felt safer with her around and—accompanied. She seemed like a canine soul mate. Which makes what I did even worse. On the first day, she began to explore the yard. She sniffed everything, every tree, every shrub, every blade of grass. She sniffed the garage and my car and the trash cans. And then she wandered into the front yard.

She began to sniff around the concrete steps, around the porch. And she began to whine. Every time I let her out, she'd make a beeline for the front porch. On the third day, she began to dig as she whined. I coaxed her back into the house, but then she whined at the front door, pawing at it, scratching. "What's the matter with Libby, Mom? Why is she doing that?" Ashley asked.

I said, "I think Libby's lonesome for her people. She probably wants to go home."

I noticed no odor coming from the porch. I'd been afraid of that, not knowing how to research the question of decaying bodies. But obviously Libby did notice. And it bothered her. So I got scared. That is the only defense I have: I was scared. Too many questions from the wrong people would inevitably lead to the discovery of my crime. There. I've said it: Crime. What I did was a crime. His death was an accident; I might have had a case for involuntary homicide. Until I tried to cover it up. Covering it up sealed my fate. At this point in time, only Libby and I knew what I'd done. And for all these years, my deepest regret is still calling the county dog catcher to come to take away my friend Libby.

On the fourth day, they came. I've tried to tell myself that, given what a wonderful creature she was, someone would have adopted her from the pound before the seven-day deadline. Or that her original owner tracked her down and took her home. I've tried very hard not to picture her being led to that gas chamber behind the pound. I've prayed every day that I did not sentence that lovely dog to her death.

So now you probably hate me. That's okay. When I think of Libby, I hate me, too.

But my sending her away was the beginning of my understanding of the choices I would have to make for the rest of my life. Think about that. Maybe tomorrow you will make a decision that will change your life. And not for the better. Anyone could. We all make hundreds of decisions every day without even being aware of them. What if one of yours means a future devoid of relationships, of having to make every next decision based on that first one? Everything I've done, or not done, since that night has been an effort to maintain that one ugly secret. Everything.

We stayed another year in that house with no more incidents to shake my comfort, such as it was. I worked at the bar to maintain an employment status and of course for living expenses. But I had plans. I'd made several thousands of dollars in the short time I'd owned my first little house without doing any fix-up at all. Then I'd bought the Lincoln Road house and had given it a major face-lift. I continued to do cosmetic repairs and a few minor structural ones. I replaced some of the less stable back porch floorboards, painted it and the trim on the windows and eaves of both house and garage.

It is truly amazing what a coat or two of paint can do to any surface. Even the stairs into the basement went from derelict to charming with a single coat of white paint that mostly soaked into the old bare wood but lightened and brightened it.

I read every book and magazine I could get my hands on to learn how to fix-up, repair, and refurbish just about anything. I asked questions of paint store and hardware clerks and butted into every conversation I overheard that had anything to do with home improvement. I cleaned and scrubbed and sanded and painted like a demon. Every extra dime and hour I had, I put into sprucing up the house. The only things I would not mess with were electricity, gas, and the roof.

Every second I spend on a ladder past the second rung is pure torture for me, so I painted the eaves with my heart in my throat, but I forced myself to do it. I painted over the dark, depressing paneling in the living room by coating it first with a primer. The kitchen cabinets were ancient metal ones with several coats of glopped-on paint. I ached for new solid wood ones, but didn't have the money, so I stripped off the old paint to get down to the bare metal. If you can't beat 'em, join 'em.

And I did all this just for us, to make our home more valuable. Resale value was foremost in my mind. I still avoided the front of the house as much as possible, but the improvements there had been done first, so I focused on the other three sides of the square. The house seemed grateful for my attentions, if that doesn't sound too weird. It was as if she were waking up from a long, neglected nap. She seemed to grow expansive, welcoming. Protective.

But other things were going on, too. I'd begun to feel confined by my own life. I was aware that I wanted more than the status quo, that I was capable of more. I relished my newly-acquired skills and found myself glancing at other fixer-uppers I drove by, assessing the amount of work needed to rehab them and the degree of my ability to do it myself. I'd always glance at the roofs first. If they looked sound, I arrogantly believed, anything else I could manage. Alone. I had to do it alone because I was determined to stay alone. Even my dear friend Becky had become a threat, for I had an overwhelming urge to confess. Except for superficial small talk with customers and co-workers, I just clammed up. I even slowly withdrew from my parents in terror of blurting out what I'd done. I avoided making new friends and avoided the old. I made sure I had a book with me at all times in order to avoid human connection. And, as part of my self-imposed punishment, I also avoided romantic encounters, even those of the briefest duration.

You'd be surprised how little sex matters once you have committed not to let it matter. I simply refused to think of it, to talk about it, to fantasize. I cut men and sex and love out of my life and poured myself into my house, my kids, my plans for my future. You don't have to believe me. You don't have to believe anything I've said. You won't get a chance to sentence me, either, as I will do that for myself, just as I did back then. I figure 20 years for my first murder. Life for my second.

I found our next house, a sad little house set back from an unpaved side road about half-way back to town. So I called about it and put our house on the market the same day. The agent who came out suggested a listing price that made my jaw drop. That, too, sounds like a cliché until you've experienced it. If I got my price, I could pay cash for the new project and have $10,000 left to start the repairs. Hell, not just start the repairs—complete them and keep a chunk of change in the bank. And that's when I got it. That's when I knew how I wanted to spend my life. I loved the physical labor, the challenge, the creative expression. And I loved buying cheap and selling dear. So that's what I did. Over and over.

Three years is the maximum time it has taken me to do a rehab, working alone for the most part, but needing to hire out some jobs to skilled, cash-strapped amateurs like me. And after each completion, sale, purchase, and move, I had more and more money socked away. I never bragged about it. I just let it quietly accumulate. I was never the ostentatious sort, anyway. My car lasted 10 years before she died. Then I paid cash for a dirt-cheap used pick-up truck that looked like hell but ran like a top with only the most minor maintenance. I needed sturdy clothes more than fashionable ones and would rather spend money on my kids than on myself. I realize now, too late, that my unconventional lifestyle took its own kind of toll on my kids, who had constantly to move and live in houses that, at first, were not particularly attractive. At least there was money for them for college. For those who chose college, that is.

And that closed the chapter on the Lincoln Road house. For awhile. I suppose you think you've heard enough. But you haven't. To understand, to truly and fully understand the decision I now have to make, you need to know some other things, about events in my early life that shaped me. Understand, I am not asking for forgiveness or pity. Not even mercy. The facts of my life are just that: facts. I don't see them as sad or pathetic or pitiable. No more so than anyone else's, at least.

To tell the truth, I have known only one person in my whole life who claimed her childhood was perfect, was ideal, with no trauma of any kind. And she is the most miserable, manipulative, despicable excuse for a human being that you would ever not want to meet. So my theory is that those of us who have survived some degree of shit are better for it. Remember that shit is just another name for manure, which makes wonderful fertilizer, which in turn encourages growth. I guess that sounds contradictory coming from a confessed murderer, but consider that until The Business With Tim, I was just another person much like you, with hopes and dreams and delights and disappointments and sorrows. So what I am asking for is just a modicum of comprehension of how I got to be the way I am.

If, after you hear the rest, you can say, "It was still wrong. What she did was wrong. I can understand, a little, how she thought or felt or reasoned, but it was still wrong. There is no excuse," then I will be able to accept that because you will be right. It will change nothing; what will be done will be done, and I will be past the point of condemnation anyway, but at least I will have had that: your understanding. So be patient with me just a while longer. Give me this one last chance to tell the story the way I believe it should be told: in my own voice and in my own way, even if it is on your time.

THE BEGINNING

S omewhere there is a photograph of me as a little
girl of two or so in a snowsuit. My dad has it, and I
wish I had a copy to show you. It is an old black
and white snapshot with scalloped edges, as if it were
cut with a pair of fancy scrap booking scissors.
Something in me wants to tell you that the snowsuit was
a pale robin's egg blue with white piping, but I don't
know if this is memory or confabulation, if I'm making
up the color to fill in a blank. Maybe I want it to have
been that color. Who knows? What I would want you to
notice about the picture is the absolute glee on my face,
the joy a little girl should have. But I have no memories
of ever feeling this way: carefree, happy, laughing. Not
one.

Every photo after this age shows a different little girl,
a guarded, cautious, joyless one. I have only photos and
documents and other people's recollections with which
to shape an image of my early life. It would be enough if

those people were reliable sources, but they have their own agendas, their own needs to remember my childhood as a happy one. They also have their own limitations, their own squeamish repressions. All I've ever needed is the truth. It didn't have to be pretty. I don't need the ruffles and flourishes. This need for the austere beauty in stark truth is one of the things that has separated me from the rest of my family.

My two brothers are examples of the two sides of my family, as much of my family as I have ever known, that is. My older brother is a dark tangle of destructive impulses. He lives not just in shadow, but in pitch darkness. And I mean this literally as well as figuratively; vampire-like, he is awake during the nights and sleeps during the days. As well, his thought processes are always negatively charged. I have never heard one positive, constructive word from him about anyone or anything. He is like a dark and heavy stone that has sunk inevitably to the bottom and dwells there.

My younger brother is the complete opposite. He is like the froth on a head of beer. Bubbly and airy, as insubstantial as a hiccup. He flits from one bright sunny spot on the pavement to the next with no sense of the importance of the balance between the sunlight and the shadow, no appreciation for the shade of self-reflection. I have never known him to follow through on even one of his myriad plans and schemes. The light shifts, and he is off again. I, on the other hand, possess all the gray tones in between. I love the sun and welcome the shadow.

Maybe this next story will explain to you the essence

of my perspective: When my daughter was a little girl of two or so, her father and I were walking with her across the parking lot of the grocery store. She stopped to admire the swirls of color in a puddle. Trying to encourage her sense of wonder, I said, "Isn't it beautiful?" Then Scott scornfully said, "Don't touch it. It's only a dirty old oil spill." And I said, "Yes, it is a dirty old oil spill. And isn't it beautiful?"

Even shit has the potential to become fertilizer to help flowers grow. So let's have a look at the shit as well as the flower. Like that. So I've asked for some truths about my life but have gotten platitudes and clichés which are like potato chips. You may have a full belly but have had no food. No real nutrition. There are huge holes in my life that no one can—or will—explain. But in truth, I know. In my heart I know. In my gut and in my bones, I know.

I have no memories before the orphanage and those are fragmented, more impression than image. The next photo I would show you, if I could, would be of my younger brother and me on the beach at Galveston. That's where the orphanage was. Neither of us is looking at the camera, as if we didn't know we were getting our pictures taken. We are both looking down and the wind is blowing my pale hair every which way. The orphanage was the good news. I was impressed by it, fascinated that we were fed three times a day—real food, not just whatever we could scavenge—and that when I hung over the edge of my neatly-made metal bed I could see all across the room, under the other beds, and the floor was so shiny I could see my reflection in it.

All the boys were in one huge room and all the girls were in another, and everything everywhere was clean and orderly. So interesting.

We were in Texas because our mother took us there, leaving our dad in Michigan without a clue where we were. Child stealing is what we call it today. Her friends were all going to Texas because that's where they lived in the winters when there was no work for them in the fields of Michigan. I don't remember any of them, not her friends and not her, either. I have a picture of her, though; she looks like my half-sister and a little like my older brother, but not like me. Sometimes I wish I did have a real memory, just one quick impression of her, but I don't. I don't remember missing her either. But wouldn't you think I would? In my mental memory box, there is a compartment labeled "Mother," but it's just an empty, messy space.

It took our dad a long time to find us and then another long time to win custody. These days, 'single parent' might mean either mother or father, but back then, it was unheard of for a man to have custody of his kids. Finally, as family lore goes, my great-aunt intervened, writing to her congresswoman to ask for help. This politician vouched for our dad, for the integrity of the family she'd known for years. So the judge relented and gave our dad custody. But my sister, my half-sister, was going somewhere else. This is what I mean about lies. I remember my sister telling me she had to go away because she was, at ten years older than me, too old to be allowed to keep living there. But then, when we were both grown, she admitted that she didn't want to go with my father because she could see that she would become a mother figure to us, that she would be expected to help raise us. But she didn't want to. My older brother told me that our dad didn't want custody of her, too, since she wasn't his blood daughter. And my younger brother said, "What sister?" So I learned that people remember what they want to in the way they want to. What and when and why and how. Memory is largely selective, and hugely unreliable.

Other memories of the orphanage are like rifling through a box of old snapshots: the kind, soft woman who was in charge of the girls who gave me a present when I had my adenoids removed. She gave me a set of miniature beauty aids: little bottles of Jergen's hand lotion, bubble bath, toilet water, which is watered-down cologne, and something else. Nail polish? I don't remember but want it to have been nail polish, a nearly transparent pink. I remember all of us being led in single file down the center stairway to the main hall to see someone named Santa. He scared me, with his odd red clothes and booming voice. I hid behind the soft woman, cried and refused to take the present he offered. I remember sand burrs that stuck to my white anklets and red canvas tennies. I remember a purple plum tree that clung against the back wall of the orphanage grounds. Now I know the name of those plums: Stanley. They were sweet and juicy and warm from the sun when we picked them fresh from the tree or off the hot sand where they fell.

I remember being taken to the beach and building

sand castles, just heaps of wet sand, really, with no significant architectural details, but we called them castles. I remember the delicious feeling of damp salty wind against my skin. And someone named Mary Ann. But I don't know who she was or why she took us to the beach. I don't remember that all the kids went, just my brothers and me. And, vaguely, I remember a long drive back to Michigan when our dad finally convinced the judge to give us to him.

Many years later, my older brother told me that our dad was pressured by his aunt to fight for custody of us, that he really didn't want to be burdened with us. But by that time, I knew my brother to be the worst kind of liar, the kind that decides the truth rather than discovers it. So I didn't believe him. Besides, I'd accidentally found a carbon copy of a letter our dad had sent to the judge. I was looking for my birth certificate and came across the decades-old letter. You'd have to know my dad to understand the impact that letter had on me.

Have you ever read in the Bible about 'stiff-necked people'?

Well, that's us. And our dad was the emperor of stiff-necked people. Proud and stiff and formal and proper. But in this letter, he was begging. Begging the judge for custody of us. Pleading. I was a little ashamed of myself for intruding on his historic privacy but also blessed to have had an opportunity to discover the truth.

For the first year or so that we moved back to Michigan, we lived with our grandparents, our dad's parents, in Muskegon. Our dad was trying to find stable employment and a place for us to live together. My memories of this time are clearer and there are more of them.

I started first grade, skipping kindergarten because my grandmother insisted to the principal that I was ready. She didn't want me to be behind the other kids my age. I lost my first tooth. I learned to break long words into smaller ones to learn to spell. And to read. Mahogany, for example, was: ma and hog and any, three little words. I still do this. One photograph I could show you to represent this period of my life was one of me in an upside-down paper plate festooned with pink crepe paper 'flowers' and tied under my chin with crepe paper ribbons. But you would have to take my word on the pinkness, as the photo is in black and white, which means of course in many shades of gray. We'd made the hats in class as costumes for a re-creation of a simplified version of a minuet, a rigidly structured, old-fashioned dance. I'd enjoyed the crafting of the costumes and the dance, too, but don't remember the educational purpose of it all. Washington's birthday? Never in a million years would I have asked. I was a quiet child, painfully shy, obedient, accepting and passive. God knows why anyone would pick on someone like me.

Perhaps it is the pack mentality, some primal instinct to drive off the injured, the injure-able, the different. For whatever reason, one of the bigger kids selected me as the object of his cruelty. One day after school this kid I didn't even know told me to put out my hand, that he had something for me. Of course, I did as he asked. Remember: obedient, accepting. But what he had for me was no present; it was a chunk of dry ice. Dry ice, paradoxically, burns. My hand was bandaged for a week, and the smell of Campho-Pheneque still has the power to take me back to that time. Another older kid, a black girl named Arnella, had taken a shine to me, as my grandmother phrased it. Arnella walked me home every day, although it was out of her way. On this day, she told my grandmother what had happened to me, but asked to be allowed to "take care of it." I didn't know what she meant, I still don't, but that bully never bothered me again. In fact, I don't remember ever seeing him again, but that doesn't mean much; I didn't know him before the incident, not even his name, and could not have identified him if asked.

Arnella kept walking me home, but she could not protect me from the bully in my own family. My older brother's chief joy throughout his life has been to torment others. Especially me. When I was little it was merely physical. He'd slam the screen door in my face and laugh at my tears. He tried to hang me from the apple tree in my grandparents' back yard, as he'd seen on the westerns on TV. My grandmother happened to glance out the window in time to save my life, but to this day I cannot abide clothing that is tight around my neck, like turtleneck sweaters or scarves in winter. Apparently there were other incidents of my older brother's meanness and of my younger brother's impulsiveness, as we shortly moved out of our grandparent's home to go live with our dad.

I haven't given you my brothers' or sister's names yet, and I'm undecided whether to. I've used fake names for my kids because I don't want you to be able to find them, at least not easily. Even after all of this is over, after I've done what I intend to do, I want them to be protected. If you know my brothers' names, you might be able to trace my kids, too. I'm sure you could anyway, if you tried hard enough, but I have no way of knowing how much time will pass before you listen to this tape. I fervently hope it is enough that the trail to my kids will be, at least, difficult. Impossible would be even better.

I mentioned my younger brother's impulsiveness. He was a sweet little kid in his own way, but his whole life has been shaped by his absolute inability to think anything through. Combined with the bull-headedness of our whole family, this trait was disastrous. One of my clearest impressions of my little brother is of him on his tricycle trying to outrun a police car.

If a door were unlocked, he'd lock it; if a drawer were shut, he'd open it. The incident with the tricycle happened after he'd let himself into a neighbor's house and turned on the gas jets. In stores, he'd be behind the counter shutting the cash drawer before anyone even realized it. It isn't so much that he made poor decisions; it's more like he didn't make decisions at all. He simply followed any impulse that occurred to him. I'm not convinced that these impulses were even at the level of true ideas that popped into his brain. I don't believe they got as far as his brain.

The closest I've come to being able to understand what his world is like was once as I was walking past a car, I had a damn near irresistible impulse to key it. This impulse came from nowhere, was based on nothing I have been able to identify, not jealousy or revenge or hostility, and it horrified me. But now I think that is what my little brother's life has been: one irresistible impulse after another. Day after month after year after decade of doing whatever occurs to him.

So I think it was just too much for our grandmother to deal with. But she didn't tell my father the truth about her decision. She told him that she was simply too old. By the time I started second grade, we moved to Mt. Pleasant.

At first we lived in what amounts to a tarpaper shack. I have a picture of this place if you don't believe me. It was one of just two remaining quickly and cheaply-assembled housing units for WPA workers during the Great Depression. We could see the concrete slabs where other units had been. All the others but one had been torn down, condemned as uninhabitable. But because of my father's military service and the unusual circumstances of his having custody of three kids, the authorities, whoever they were, allowed us temporary residence. My memories of this place are few but bleak indeed. Dismal one bedroom, scavenged furniture, dilapidation, hopelessness, dismay. As if the very building had absorbed the despair of all its previous occupants. We crowded in as best we could, sleeping on canvas and wood army cots, and I try not to think about who watched us as he worked; I remember no one. One pleasurable memory was of wandering in a shady, wooded area and playing with plants that looked like umbrellas. Now I know the name of that plant:

Mayapple. So I was what? Seven? And I had already discovered the pleasure of solitude.

We didn't live there long, though. Soon we moved into the upstairs of a red brick house that had been divided into apartments. I didn't know it at the time, but my grandparents had bought this house. The rent from the downstairs apartment paid the mortgage. I have a picture of this place, too, also in black and white, but I don't need a picture to remember. Still not anything like attractive, this house was a definite improvement over the shack.

This move was just before my second-grade year. My memories of this house on the corner of Oak and Cherry are more like a slide show than a photograph album: Three twin beds around three walls of the room we three kids shared. An icebox on the back porch into which a huge clear block of ice fit into perfectly. Our dad's attempt at homemade beer that went terribly wrong, creating a smelly yellow cascade down the back stairs. Staying up past bedtime to listen to the election results and rejoicing because our dad rejoiced at the announcement; he would always be on the side of the military man. A babysitter named Dawn who taught me to embroider to keep me out of her hair so she could write her endless letters to her boyfriend in the Navy. I should say she taught me to tear out embroidery because she was a perfectionist and highly critical of my childish attempts at needlework.

My second grade teacher who seemingly willingly sat patiently with me during recesses trying and trying and trying to teach me to tell time on a cardboard circle 'dial' with two brass-fastened cardboard hands and big black numbers. I struggled and struggled for even the slightest progress which I promptly forgot. By our next session, she would patiently start all over. Eventually, I caught on, but not without regret; I'd enjoyed the feminine attention that I did not have at home.

I also remember playing 'horses' with my friend Janeen: on our hands and knees, we would 'graze' during recess, actually eating grass and the little buttons of a plant that grew prolifically on the school grounds. I've never been able to identify that plant, and it now feels weird to say that, that we ate grass and weeds. Good grief, we could have gotten sick or even died. But we didn't. We professed to like the taste, but I've tried them since because I found the same weed growing in my yard and remembered eating those round, flat little seeds. They really don't taste like anything much.

Another olfactory memory (besides the beer cascade) was of frying onions. My dad, I think, put onions in everything. I still do. My final memory is of falling asleep while reading my first chapter book, Little Women. Trying to encourage reading, my dad had enrolled me in a children's book club, so every month I would receive in the mail a new book that was all my own. They even came addressed to me. Little Women was my first, and I dove in eagerly, lying on my cot by the window. When I awoke, the apartment was empty and terrifyingly quiet. I cautiously explored all four rooms, but no one was there. In a household of mostly male people, it is never quiet. Boys seem to need noise on a cellular level. Not even the radio was playing. I crawled back into my bed and clutched my book, afraid even to think, afraid to wonder. I sent my consciousness into my fear deeper and deeper until my dad and brothers came home. It was probably only a few minutes; that's what Daddy told me. He hadn't wanted to wake me from my reading-induced slumber, but needed something from the hardware store, so he left me by myself. He explained this as he held me, consoling me as I sobbed my relief at his return. Loss and abandonment were then and are still my triggers. But I cry only after the fact, after the crisis is over. Until then, I send myself into myself, into my fear.

I'll bet you are thinking: "Good grief, is she going to give us a blow-by-blow account of her childhood?" I'm not. I couldn't if I wanted to. Could anyone? Could you? All any of us have are handfuls of images, visual, auditory, gustatory, and olfactory, to represent our early years.

But I do not think they are random. I recently heard (but can't verify) it's been proven that humans are incapable of truly random acts. I haven't had time to explore this theory, and I guess I won't have, but it intrigues me. Every act by every human, however random it may seem, is a culmination of learned responses and deliberation? Of split-second decisions based on multiple factors such as past events and anticipated consequences and projected probabilities? Fascination. I wish I had more time to toy with these ideas, to explore this theory. To read about it, to learn something, to challenge the theory and myself. But I don't.

However, if it is true, it supports my thoughts about memory: it is, by nature, selective. And representative. That one memory of the first time I remember being left alone in representative of all the times I've been left alone, and it is representative also of how I would handle future events, would be an indicator of something inherent in my character. And as an indicator, it serves also as a predictor. How I first learned to withdraw to survive is what interests me.

I'm sorry. I'll try to stay focused. It's the wrong question, anyway. How could any human being take the life of another?

That's the question. Especially considering that person had spent her entire life until that point being protective of the smaller and weaker of any species. Kittens, especially. I collected kittens: pictures of them and calendars featuring them and little china figurines of them and occasionally the living variety. If I found one, lost or injured, I'd bring it home and ask my dad to let me keep her. In my childish heart, kittens were always 'her' regardless of their biological sex. Daddy always said, "No" at first, then "Just until morning," then "Well, I guess so, if you take care of it." I would pet them and cuddle them and breathe in the essential kitten-ness of them as I fell asleep with them curled up on my pillow with my nose buried in their soft purring necks. And always, after a few days, they would disappear as if I'd imagined them. Perhaps I believed they'd wandered off or vaguely suspected my daddy had found better homes for them. It never would have occurred to my innocent and trusting heart that anything truly bad might have happened to any of them. It would very simply never have entered my mind.

We moved again. And again. And again. By the time I was in the tenth grade, we'd moved ten times and I'd gone to ten different schools. My dad would lose his job, then get a better one, and off we'd go.

I remember each house we lived in and have those requisite handful of memories from each school. A photo album of the third grade would feature Alma, Spanish for 'soul,' and would include the first time I had my own room and a cherry tree in the back yard, from which my dad made a cherry pie in a long baking dish because we didn't have a pie pan. A peach tree, also in the back yard, yielded only a few hard and tasteless fruits. An alluring expanse of neatly clipped grass and stately pine trees behind the house, which was the grounds of the veteran's home that abutted the residential area. A whole wall of aptly named 'four o'clocks' that bloomed in the late afternoon.

The woven grasscloth on one whole wall of the dining room and against which my father placed his desk. The irritation of the mustache he grew that year and that I kiss-boycotted until he shaved it off. The Shillings across the street.

Mrs. Shilling watched us after school until my dad got home. She taught me to iron and to make her son's bed. On my first solo attempt, I mismade it, putting the top edge of the chenille bedspread at the bottom. I remember her son's scathing ridicule of me, her scolding of him, and my deep humiliation. And I remember Mr. Shilling's tongue that he mysteriously thrust into my mouth when I dutifully kissed him goodbye as my father told me to. It was so odd, so repulsive, that habit of his. His tongue was fat and slimy and I had no idea why he did that. My daddy didn't kiss me like that, neither did my grandpa; no one else did. I wish now that I'd asked in a loud voice, "Daddy, why does Mr. Shilling stick his tongue in my mouth?" I wish now I'd blown the whistle. Because I know now why he did that, and I can clearly imagine what else he might have done if he'd had a chance. But at the time, it was only confusing and gross. So I never told my dad. And I never asked my brothers if he did the same wet, fat tongue thing with them, too.

Was I already conditioned to keep the secrets of men? Conditioned to silent endurance? Of complicity? Of acquiescence? Of submission? Of tolerance of the intolerable?

People called me shy, but now I wonder about that shyness. Is shyness a mask for helplessness? For an impoverished spirit?

Also while in the third grade, I learned that girls could betray me, too. For the first time in my life, I was allowed the absolute delight of having a girlfriend come over. Janet was a classmate, and we'd made friends quickly. As all children do, I enjoyed showing her my things: the ancient dark wood chest my grandpa had given me to put my treasures in; letters from my grandma; a set of silk neck scarves in every color of the rainbow that my great-aunt had given me; a broken beaded bracelet that I'd found in the trash behind Mrs. Shilling's house, and my most prized possession of all: my Cinderella watch with its blue leather band that my daddy bought for me as a reward for learning to tell time.

Janet admired my watch and tried it on, then put it back. I thought. We then played with my ever-growing doll collection until it was time for her to go home. I refused to believe the obvious when my watch came up missing. A friend would not do that. A friend could not do that. But she had. She confessed later the next week when my smashed watch was found on the playground. Losing my watch was less painful than losing my friend and yet another sliver of my ability to trust.

Are you thinking: "What the hell does any of this have to do with murder"? I wouldn't blame you. And I have no answer. I have no clue why these things seem important, why I feel compelled to tell you all of this. Maybe we will both understand better later. Maybe it will be like putting together a 500-piece jigsaw puzzle: at first it is a meaningless jumble of color and shape, but eventually, piece by piece, the full picture starts to emerge, starts to make sense. Unless, of course, there is a key piece missing.

We moved again, away from Mr. Shilling's tonguey kisses. We moved back to Muskegon, to my dad's hometown, back to where my grandparents lived. I was so happy that we would be able to see them more often, and even when we couldn't, it was comforting to know they were not far away.

This would be the longest time we'd be in one place. From the fourth through the beginning of my seventh grades, we lived in a housing project. Four two-story units made up the building we lived in. It was flanked by two six-unit buildings, each of which featured a one-story bungalow at each end. These three buildings made an elongated U, which was repeated many times along the rear of the project. Although the word 'project' has gained a mostly negative connotation, at the time it provided affordable housing, ample playmates, and the distinct advantage of private ownership. For, although our unit was one thin wall from the next, it was our own. Again I had my own room, this time upstairs.

My school years there are one dull gray blur with few events of significance. I remember learning to square dance, this school's version of physical education, I suppose. I remember collecting the cardboard discs from our daily pints of warmish milk in their charming little glass bottles, but I haven't a clue why I collected them. Sometimes I walk into a small country store and am hit with the same sour smell of those pints of milk. I remember digging holes in the playground with my heels to make the pot for a game of marbles, but don't remember how we played, what the rules were. I remember winning a lot of marbles and carrying them to school in a tin lard pail with a wire handle, but not where I got the tin. I remember dozing off when my only male teacher to that point would lecture. His monotone and the stuffiness of the room never failed to relax me—too much.

I remember music education classes that took place in the lunch room. Music education was really just a sing-along, but I enjoyed the break from times tables and states' capitols. We learned "Down in the Valley" and "Picking Up Paw Paws" and "Nobody Knows the Trouble I've Seen" and "White Coral Bells." I still remember all the words to these songs, and one more. We learned all the verses to a mournful song about being a motherless child. And I began to wonder. What exactly was so bad about being a motherless child? My brothers and I were motherless children. Was I supposed to be mournful, too?

Before we learned this song, I had not questioned our single-parent family structure, although that term had not yet been coined. My dad was raising us three kids on his own. It was just a fact that I accepted. Of course I was aware that we were different, the neighborhood freaks wherever we lived. I knew that some people—women, mostly—had an odd pitying expression on their faces when they spoke to us kids, especially to me. I knew that most of my friends had a father and a mother but didn't see how that benefited them, didn't see how that made their lives any better than ours—or them any better than us. To illustrate my attitude, a friend once asked what I suppose many wondered: "What's it like to not have a mom?"

Without any rancor, I quickly responded, "What's it like to have one?" Then my friend and I just sat there, side by side on the steps of our unit, imagining.

Their dads got up in the morning, got themselves

ready for work, then left to earn their daily bread; my dad got himself up in the morning, got us up, got himself ready for work, got us ready for school, packed our lunches, sent us off, then left for his job. After school, my friends went home to a mom who told them to go outside to play; after school, we went home to an empty house then went outside to play. As the afternoon wore on, cooking smells pervaded the neighborhood as moms prepared dinners. Late in the afternoons or early in the evenings, my friends' dads would come home and then my friends would be called in for dinner. Our dad would come home and start dinner and then call us in to eat. After dinner, all the other kids would go back outside to play until darkness sent them inside. We kids could go outside, too, after we'd done the dishes. But as I recall, the ten or fifteen minute job doing the dishes should have been usually took hours as we'd dawdle and squabble and fiddle-fart around until it was too late to go back out. On Saturdays and Sundays, the differences were more pronounced.

On Saturdays, my friends would be sent outside to play, but we had chores to do, simple things at first, like folding laundry or dusting, then progressing to sweeping and mopping. We had to clean our own rooms, but I use the word 'clean' rather loosely. What my brothers were usually doing was more squabbling, but my favorite housekeeping activity was to rearrange my room. The bed under the window? No, against the door? No, against the west wall? The east?

For a while we had a cleaning lady. Once a week we

would come home from school to the overpowering reek of Pine Sol, her cleaning agent of choice. She must have used a quart a day, the smell was so strong. But even to my childish eyes, it was clear that the house was much improved from her efforts. Everything sparkled. For a day or two, at least.

On Sundays, we went to church. As far as I ever knew, we were the only family to go to church every week. Every week. I remember only one Sunday we didn't go because Daddy was sick. Pale and shivering, he lay on the couch fending off some virus, I suppose. At the time I was terrified. What if I lost my Daddy? What if he died? He was the center of my world, my tower of strength with an immune system that could kill rats in the next county. He would pull me onto his lap and put his arms around me and every slight of any thoughtless friend, every meanness of an older brother, every hurt or ache would magically disappear. In my Daddy's arms, I was safe. No one and nothing could hurt me there. In his arms I was home.

But my friends seemed not even to know their daddies. They seemed almost not to like their dads or to be afraid of them. Many of my friends had daddies who would come home in drunken rages, or who might not come home at all. Some of my friends' fathers didn't even go to work but sat at home all day long drinking beer and watching television. Some of those daddies didn't even get dressed in the morning, but stayed in their pajamas. It was very odd.

Some of the mothers would try to mother me, and some of my teachers would, too. But my dad would always say, "Let them get their own little girls" and reject their overtures. Once he relented, though, and let my fourth-grade teacher, Miss Givens, take me home to have dinner with her. I was stiff and silent most of the time as she tried to engage me in conversation over dinner. I enjoyed the experience but must've not shown it because she never asked me again. Maybe she didn't enjoy it. Who knows? Unless it was my grandmother or one of the great-aunts, I was uncomfortable around women. So why did I start to pray for a mom?

I blame those song lyrics: "Sometimes I feel like a motherless child." Something about the sorrow and hopelessness expressed in those words made me start thinking maybe I needed a mother after all, even if I couldn't quite figure out what for. So every night as I knelt by my bed and said my Now-I-Lay-Me-Down-To-Sleeps, I finished with the simple request for a mother.

And I did this for years until God decided to respond by teaching me the meaning of, "Be careful what you ask for; you just might get it." Maybe He wanted just to teach me to be very, very specific when I pray.

But that came later. For this period, the definitive photo I'd share with you is of me standing on the back steps. I'm wearing slacks that I don't remember, a zippered jacket that I do remember—blue and green plaid on a white background—the ubiquitous canvas sneakers. In the photo, my hair is short and frizzy from the perm my dad had given me. Obscuring much of my face is a huge pink bubble I'd blown with my bubble gum, and dangling from my right wrist is my beloved red plastic Brownie box camera. You'll have to take my word for the colors of these items because the photo is black and white. I especially love this photo because it is obvious in the squint of my eyes above the bubble that I was happy in that moment. Just a kid, ten or eleven, relaxed and happy. But beneath that jacket were the beginnings of the breasts that would ruin my childhood and my ability to relax, to be happy.

Do you think we tend to love activities at which we excel, or is it the other way around: that we get excellent at activities we love? In school, I loved anything to do with reading, but I was learning more than history and geography and English. I was learning also about human nature. For example, I remember Mickey. He was a fat boy who played percussion with me in our sixth-grade band. Mickey knew I preferred the bass drum to the snare, so he always deferred to me although he loved the bass, too. He was a sweet kid, gentle and shy and thoughtful, but his chubbiness made him the brunt of much playground teasing and petty, childish taunts. Suddenly he stopped coming to school, and after a while, we learned he'd died of something called leukemia. All of a sudden, the same kids who'd tormented him were crying and carrying on about the loss of their "friend."I was sickened by this, my first understanding of the word "hypocrisy."

I remember Garan, too. A friend of my older brother, he came from a family my father considered questionable. There were rumors of trouble with the law, and founded or unfounded, "trouble with the law" was no badge of courage or coolness, especially with my dad. I am surprised that my brother was allowed to play with Garan, but perhaps Daddy didn't realize how much time they spent together.

Garan, for some bizarre reason, had a crush on me. If one of his friends had a crush on me, my older brother would do all he could to encourage it, throwing questionable boys in my path at any opportunity.

Garan did his utmost to gain my attention, to impress me, from riding his bicycle standing up and with no hands to chasing me, literally, throughout the neighborhood. Finally, in school one day he chased me with a wire coat hanger. When I tripped and fell, he did, too, and the raw wire tip of the coat hanger ripped across my left eyelid. I wore a dramatic, attention-getting eye patch while the cut healed shut and still have the scar.

My revenge was off school grounds, simple and clean. I walked up to Garan, balled up my right fist and let him have it right in the gut. One shot. He doubled over and dropped to the ground, writhing and crying. "Why did you do that?" he sobbed, tears mingling with snot, "I have a glass stomach."

I still don't know what a glass stomach is, but I learned two things in that brief exchange of power. I learned that bullies are easy to bully. And I learned that unexpected violence is more effective than expected. I hadn't even hit him that hard. Garan was taller and stronger. But down he went. As much as possible, I believe in settling things without the use of violence. But sometimes we have to speak to people in a language they will understand. Reasoning with Garan would never have worked. He would never have apologized if I hadn't punched him. But he did afterward. I, however, never did.

My father was appalled. He was trying so hard to raise me to be a lady. But really, what were the odds of that? He dressed me in frilly dresses, pretty hats, and white gloves to go to church every Sunday morning. He would never take me to the store with him (or anywhere in public, as a matter of fact) unless I changed out of slacks and into a skirt. He gave me perms so my impossibly straight and willful (or won't-ful) hair would curl femininely. And he bought me all the dolls my room would hold. And there I was punching out the neighborhood bully, an older boy whose family was of questionable character. What next?

Next was on its way.

We neighborhood kids decided to put on a carnival to raise money. For what, I do not know. For sure it was not some worthy cause such as UNICEF, for which we dutifully carried cardboard canisters each Halloween in which we collected mostly pennies. This, of course, was in addition to, not instead of, our traditional pillowcase for more immediate and physical gratifications. And by "we kids," I mean the kids of our U: twelve or fifteen of us of various ages and imaginations.

At an organizational meeting on the Schneiders' stoop (two doors down at the end unit), we shared our ideas for events for the carnival: apple dunking in Mr. Schneider's galvanized steel bucket; a fish pond with paper fish on cotton string hung from sticks;

PickPocket the clown costume sewn with multiple pockets in which could be placed a trinket of some sort. Then I shared my idea, which I thought close to brilliant. I would, I suggested, dance to some music we'd play on Lois McRae's record player and take off one piece of clothing at a time. The other kids thought it was a great idea and were proposing various songs when Mrs. Schneider made her indignant presence known. For some reason she objected—strenuously—to my contribution.

I can only imagine my dad's reaction when he was informed of his only daughter's ambition, but needless to say, I did not perform in that particular fashion. Ignominiously, I played the part of PickPocket the Clown as I was the only one with the skill to sew many, many pockets on a pair of someone's dad's castoff coveralls. For a nickel, someone could fish a penny gumball charm out of one of my pockets. And there was no music.

How I knew of such things as strippers is another story and not nearly as salacious as I'm sure the neighborhood mothers imagined.

When we went on long car rides, our dad would keep us busy (and probably distracted from our favorite pastime of tormenting each other) by singing songs. I know, I know, everybody's parents do that. By my dad was just a little different in his musical selections.

Instead of "Old McDonald Had a Farm" or "There Was a Farmer Who Had A Dog And Bingo Was His Name-O," my dad taught us songs about a Zulu warrior and waltzing with Matilda and the Marine Corps Hymn and someone named Yon Yonson who came from Visconsin and someone named Queenie, the queen of the burlesque show.

With my typical childish innocence and curiosity, I asked my dad what the burlesque show was. With his typical candor, he explained that the song was about a stripper. So then, of course, I needed to know what a stripper was. But then he got uncomfortable and wouldn't tell me. All he'd say was that he'd explain it one day. This response was supposed to appease me, but never did. Instead, it inevitably drove me to his foot-thick Webster's Unabridged Dictionary, perfectly good reading material when all my school and library books had been read up.

We also had an absolutely fascinating medical guide, a set of Funk and Wagnall's Encyclopedias he'd bought one volume a week at the grocery store, and as many books as would fit on the brick and glass-shelved bookcase he'd built. We had lots of other weird things, too, things that fascinated my friends who had mothers and so were, presumably, deprived of such things.

For instance, when we needed a new sofa but couldn't afford one, my frugal but creative father bought a bolt of black denim and re-covered our old one. We had a jute area rug and bamboo roll-up blinds that my dad said reminded him of the South Pacific where he'd served in the military during WWII.

We had a record player, not in itself an unusual item, but the records we had certainly puzzled my friends. We had music of other countries and times and cultures. We had military music; we had classical music; we had spiritual music; and we had beer drinking music, mostly German.

But the strangest item of all, at least to my friends, was the big black iron Underwood typewriter that sat on my dad's desk. He wrote a monthly column for a military magazine, so for at least one night a month I fell asleep to the tap dance of the Underwood's keys.

Most nights I fell asleep to classical music. I still drift off when I hear Haydn. I realize now that my dad was using a kind of musical control strategy. At night, classical music effectively defused us kids' exuberant energies. On Friday nights, when we sometimes had pizza, the drinking songs set a party tone. On Saturday mornings, when there were chores to be done, the rousing strains of John Phillip Sousa and his ilk set the tone for get-up-and-get-to-work. On Sunday mornings, spirituals and hymns accompanied our preparations for early service. I am still acutely aware of the power of music to set, amplify, or alter a mood.

Recently, my dad asked me if I'd had a happy childhood. I didn't know what to say. Is there such a thing? Or, aren't they all? I have happy memories. And sad ones.

Good ones and bad ones. Isn't that the norm? Our family situation wasn't exactly normal, wasn't within the reasonably predictable 67 percent experienced by families of the time, but I've known only that one person who has claimed a normal childhood. So doesn't that mean abnormal becomes the norm? Like most of the boys I knew, my older brother had a mean streak and my younger brother was fun to be around. Except for the aberrant cultural influences we were exposed to, we were as normal as anyone I knew. Until the latter part of my sixth grade, that is. But for all I know, the ugliness is normal, too.

By the end of my sixth grade, I was the only girl in my class who didn't wear a bra but the only one who needed one. Except for my clothes not fitting the same anymore, I didn't feel much different. But other people started acting differently around me. Boys and girls began to speak to my chest instead of my face. Sometimes they'd just stare, forgetting to speak at all. I tried to hide my swelling chest under loose, heavy sweaters and jackets or by carrying my books clutched to my chest. Or by slouching. But I couldn't hide behind things all the time, especially at home, where this uninvited attention was worst.

At home, my older brother, who before this had just been mean as a snake, became as dangerous as one, too. If I came anywhere within arm's reach, he was reaching. He'd grab, poke, pinch, and squeeze my rapidly-expanding chest at every opportunity.

Before long, he added verbal to physical by begging, pleading, bribing, threatening, ordering me to let him see them. To let him touch them, fondle them. He knew the rules of privacy our dad had imposed. He knew my room was off limits. He knew he was supposed to knock and get permission before entering my room or the bathroom if someone else were in it. But he started knocking after he'd open the door, especially if I were dressing or in the bathtub. If he could get close enough, he'd try to look down my shirts. I learned quickly to keep far from him, to put a chair under a doorknob to act as a lock, to stuff my door's keyhole with cotton after one night when I'd caught him peeking through it. I started avoiding looking at people directly in their eyes so I wouldn't have to see where their eyes were looking. But it got worse.

Wait. I know what you're thinking: why didn't you tell your dad? And I don't know the answer, not even now, when it's been decades since I've been willing to be in the same room with my brother and I've had so much time to try to understand why I did or did not do things that so influenced my life. Part of it may be that even as a kid I was aware of the pressure my dad was under as a single dad way back then. I knew he lived under constant social scrutiny and judgment and fear that, like our mother before him, he just might lose custody of us if he messed up. Or if we did. And part of it may be my own fear of my brother's evil sense of retribution.

My brother, in the seventh or eighth grade at the time, once confided in me that he was plotting to kill a girl in his school who would not return the interest he had in her, would not go out with him. By the specificity of his plans, I came to believe he was entirely capable of doing it. How much worse would it be for me, a mere sister, if I told? And then there is that same reticence, natural or induced, that kept me from telling on Mr. Schilling and his icky tongue. And part of that, now that I think about it, may be a form of magical thinking: If I never speak of it, it didn't really happen. The unspoken secret has no more substance than a nightmare. But of course, I now, too late, realize that even nightmares need to be spoken of, need to be examined and analyzed and labeled and categorized, must be understood to be eradicated. Too late. Too late.

We moved again a few weeks into my seventh grade. Before we moved, our housekeeper had bought me a few bras. She'd guessed at a size, but the cups were too small. Still, tucked into a bra, which was uncomfortable at first and difficult to get into the habit of wearing, I felt less vulnerable. One more layer of cloth between my flesh and my brother's obsessive grasp. One more layer of protection between me and those prying eyes. And then, too, I felt more grown-up in a bra. I finally understood why all my little flat-chested friends had been so proud of their cupless training bras.

Remember when I was talking about memory, about the big red brick house we'd lived in on Gratiot Road near Saginaw? That is the house we moved to. I have no photo to show you of that period, only mental ones, but they are mostly black and white, except of course for the house itself and the barn behind it.

I was sad to be a two-hour drive from my grandparents, but Daddy had promised we'd go home once a month to visit for a whole weekend. And I loved the house itself. The rooms were spacious, with high ceilings and wide glowing woodwork and hardwood floors. The house felt gracious, somehow, solid and stable. I would have loved to stay there, for that home to be my claim to a real home, one we wouldn't have to leave. And now, because of numerology, I understand why: That house was a 4, the very number of solidity and stability. No wonder I loved it. Even then I longed for just those qualities.

But it was also this house that I associate with one of the most emotionally painful events of my life, an event that marked me permanently.

You get it, right? That I was a complete Daddy's girl? My Daddy was my world. He could do no wrong. In this way, all Daddy's girls are the same. My Daddy hung the moon, called up the sun, and changed the seasons. The brightest spot of any day was when he came home and I could run into his arms. He would scoop me up and hug me and ask, "How is my little girl?" How is my little girl. My little girl. The sweetest words I've ever known. But long gone.

One day my daddy came home and I ran to greet him, as always. But this day I was wearing one of my new bras, too tight and too small, but protective. I ran to my daddy's arms, laughing with my accustomed delight to have him home, to have him back. I was no sooner in his arms than I was right back out again. He'd thrust me away from him in absolute disgust.

"What are you wearing? What the hell do you have on?" he shouted at me.

"A bra," I admitted, never dreaming it was an object of revulsion.

"Where did you get it?"

"Mrs. McGee bought it for me," I confessed.

"Judas Priest. That damned, interfering god-damned woman. Take it off. Get right upstairs and take it off.

Right now."

And of course, I did. Shamed and confused, I barely spoke that night. Or for many more. Eventually he must have gone to his mother, my grandmother, with his problem, as she took me aside and explained that my dad was afraid of losing his little girl and so had over-reacted. It was perfectly all right to wear a bra, she said. She wore one.

But the damage was done. I had grown the god-damned breasts and now, by God, now I had to live with them. I never ran to greet him again, and he never again hugged me or called me his little girl. I went from Daddy's little girl to nobody's girl in a heartbeat.

With no idea whatsoever what to do with my hurt, no one to go to, no one to love me or accept me just the way I was, horrid breasts and all, I turned to my one remaining but ever true friend: books. I read anything and everything I could get my hands on. I read voraciously, seeking between the covers of books a place to belong. For the hours I could escape into a book, I could align my identity with whoever was the heroine du jour. I could live other lives in other worlds and other times and feel other pains and fears than my own. And I learned that with my nose stuck inside a book I was safe. My brothers left me alone. My father left me alone. The whole world went away, and I was left deliciously alone—with my books. And when I wasn't reading, I was writing dark poems about death and dying and being buried at sea. Reading and writing: nothing else interested me.

I remember one night watching with my father an

apparently side-splitting television show. He was roaring with laughter, tears literally streaming down his cheeks. Then he looked at me sitting deadpan nearby. The humor had completely escaped me.

Disgusted, he said, "Why are you so damned blasé?"

Of course, I looked up the definition of that word, too. But I wasn't that at all. I wasn't blasé; I was worse. Much worse. I was dead inside. Disconnected.

I felt far away from everyone else; they even looked far away, small somehow and insignificant, their voices muffled and faint. I was wrapped in an impenetrable cocoon of complete lack of feeling, good or bad. And I was helpless to do anything about it.

Not at least until I learned the power of my unasked-for metamorphosis from precious little girl to god-damned woman could give me. My father was clearly unprepared for the changes my body was going through, and quite naturally my breasts were not the half of it. My periods started. Prompted, no doubt by the bra episode, my grandmother had sent for a starter kit of sanitary napkins and a sketchily-illustrated booklet explaining the impending menses. She slipped the kit to me during one of our monthly visits (no play on words intended). "Don't let your daddy see this," she'd whispered, as duplicitous as any international spy.

Reading was reading, so I read the booklet carefully, three times at least, then hunkered down for the onslaught. I was prepared for the possibility of cramps, which the booklet had warned of. And for all her whispered admonishments, my grandmother must have prepared my father as well, for shortly after her delivery of my starter kit, I complained of not feeling well. "Ah," he'd said, knowingly, "growing pains."

As I hadn't grown (at least in height) since sixth grade, an eon of a year before, I did not at first recognize the euphemism when I heard it. But soon I learned the code. And the power of the code. My father's squeamishness about all things female made him the perfect patsy for my soon-to-be-perfected malingering.

If I didn't feel like going to school (and I often didn't feel like going to school) all I had to do was fake a bout of menstrual cramps. A little groaning, a little clutching of my abdomen, and my father would get visibly nervous, would mutter something about growing pains, and hoping I'd feel better. Then out the door he'd go, leaving me sweetly, deliciously alone in the big old house. I'd go back to bed until 10 or 11, get up and eat some cereal or peanut butter toast, read or watch TV. My favorite school-skipping program was on a local educational television channel. I enjoyed learning about art, about perspective drawing, about shading and proportion and white space. I fell in love with the entire concept of white space. To draw what wasn't there was such an exciting idea. To focus on the spaces between things in order to portray what was exhilarated me. Being right handed, I drew my left endlessly, in every imaginable pose and was so deeply gratified that those hands looked exactly like my own. Amazing.

It isn't that I really minded school, it simply didn't interest me.

Oddly enough, my teachers were not encouraging of

my habit of reading and discouraged it in classes. So I began to read all night, then attend school in a sleep-deprived fog. I most enjoyed my French class because it wasn't really a class; we spent most of our time at computers with headsets, learning alone and at our own speeds. It was an experimental program, as were many of my other classes, and the novelty of the curriculum had just begun to penetrate my fog when we moved again. Back to Mt. Pleasant and the house we'd lived in during my second grade, back to the apartment house my grandparents had bought and still owned.

We moved suddenly and silently in the middle of the night. I still have no idea why we moved or why we moved the way we did. I've never asked, assuming always that I would get the typical non-answer. One school day, my father came home early from work and told us to get everything packed; we were moving. No goodbyes to friends or teachers, no apologies or explanations. Just pack up and go. So we did.

This time we lived in the downstairs apartment. Our old upstairs one was occupied by renters that I do not remember at all. It should have been a pleasant experience, going home in a way. But it wasn't. For one thing, my dad had moved us but not his job. So he came home only on the weekends, leaving us to fend for ourselves during the week. It wasn't as neglectful as it sounds; he'd arranged for a line of credit with a neighborhood store, so we kids could buy what we needed during the week, and he would pay for it on Saturdays.

Okay, saying it out like that makes him sound like a

bad parent, but he must have been under extreme duress to take such measures. He always did the best he could for us; he even frequently said that raising us alone wasn't a burden. It was a privilege. That's the word he used: privilege. And he had no way of knowing what I was going through because I never told him. I didn't have the feelings of trust I'd had when I was younger, and I was afraid of the consequences.

My older brother, completely free of the constraints of a clear and present parent, stepped up his attentions to me, to my breasts. He would not pass by me without "accidentally" brushing against or falling into my chest. His occasional insincere apologies were always accompanied by a smirk. I had already learned to jam a chair under my bedroom door's knob at night and to assess his location before stepping out of my room. And now I learned other tactics to avoid him. I learned to leave for school early and to carry my books clutched in front of me. I learned to go home after school by cutting through people's side and back yards in order to get home enough before him to take fast showers. There was no lock on the bathroom door and he'd left off the pretense of knocking.

I still wore oversized sweaters, bulky jackets. I stuffed a flannel sheet blanket under the crack at the bottom of the door but still undressed under the covers or with my back turned toward the door and the window. I avoided his presence with every tactic I could imagine, relaxing my guard only on the weekends when my father, our father, was home. Fortunately, this period did not last long.

One of the things my dad was doing back in Saginaw on weekdays, besides working of course, was searching for a new home for us. Just what I wanted, and badly. But as is often the case, just what I wanted in the worst way is just the way I got it. He was excited and happy with the solution he hit upon. I was appalled. It was brand new, and it was ours. But it was 12'x55': a white and aqua Marlette trailer. I know, I know, they were and are called mobile homes. But to me it was and always will be a trailer. We rented a lot at the end of a dead end street only a mile or so from the roomy red brick house I'd loved. There were six, maybe seven other mobile homes back there; it wasn't like a modern trailer park, but I hated it anyway. My room was smaller than tiny, my closet had two built-in drawers beneath it and was smaller than a small shower stall. My twin bed took up half the room's width and its entire length. I had one tiny window too high up on the wall to look out of or to allow sunlight in, and it was flush with the wall with no ledge, so no arranging my girlish trinkets there. As there was no room to display or store them, my collection of rocks in jars of water to enhance their colors was left behind. My extensive doll collection (I'd had a hundred at one point) went across state into my grandmother's attic. But I refused to give up my books. These I stored in boxes short enough to slide under my bed.

The only advantages of living there that I would acknowledge were that my dad came home every night, no one could peek through my window, and the acoustics were so sensitive that I knew at every minute where my brother was. The boob-grabbing and sly suggestions lessened considerably, but his ugly impulses took a nasty turn.

I don't want to talk about this. I'm trying to find some 'round-about way to tell you, and I wouldn't at all if I didn't think it was significant. It might have something to do with The Business With Tim, with my ability to off a bully.

Times are different now. Now the garbage men come around every Monday morning, Tuesday if Monday is a holiday. But back then we burned our trash. Everyone I knew did. We had a burn barrel, usually an old rusty 55 gallon steel drum with punctures through the walls near the bottom for air to circulate. Fire needs air, you know.

My dad, as I've mentioned, is former military. I don't mean to repeat myself or to bore you with needless details. I know you've thought I'm just stalling, buying time with all of this. I know you have. But it matters. All of it. It matters. Anyway, the best my dad knew of raising kids was like training troops. So we had a duty roster instead of a chores list. For the most part, it was a weekly rotating roster; we were all expected to do dishes, to sweep, to vacuum, to dust, to scour sinks. Then we had inspection. If our chore-of-the-week wasn't done to our dad's satisfaction, we had to do it over. And quite possibly over again, until he approved.

I don't think it hurt any of us to learn to keep our home clean, to be responsible. For sure it eliminated the concept of woman's work. In the military and in our house, there was simply work and it all needed to be done.

Some chores, however, were not rotating. Burning the trash was my older brother's chore, although any time there was a fire, the other two of us could be counted on to be drawn to it. Human nature or budding pyros? Who knows?

A mean streak is one thing, but my older brother had more of a wide swath of cruelty. If he had a kind streak, I never saw it. Besides the fixation with my body, he never missed an opportunity to disparage, insult, or ridicule another person. He seemed to take special delight in putting our little brother up to some ridiculous stunt, then sit back and grin when our dad would lambaste the poor, gullible, impulsive little kid.

We are no longer close, but when we were kids together, I was as protective of my little brother as I dared to be. My fear of my older brother's revenge kept me from telling my dad the truth about most of his escapades: He'd been our older brother's dupe. I just noticed I said I "was" protective, but realize I've not included him much in all this. So I'm still doing it. My anger toward him, my disappointment, I suppose, was still in the future.

Where the kitten came from, I don't remember. Unwanted kittens seem to be a recurring theme in my life. I've often thought that if I ever won the lottery I'd start a program to help people spay or neuter their pets. It is so expensive, I know, that even enlightened pet owners with the very best of intentions hesitate to get it done. But the pain and suffering of all the neglected, thrown-away puppies and kittens must be worth something, aren't they? So they starve to death or get hit by cars or get worms or some disease or other, or they get bled to death by fleas or ticks. Or they die excruciating deaths at the hands of innumerable human monsters just having a little fun.

My older brother was just having a little fun when he put the kitten in a plastic pail and swung it around and around until the kitten involuntarily shit in it.

Centrifugal force, my brother explained. But it was no pseudo-science lesson when he unbent a wire coat hanger and rammed it up the kitten's anus.

The trash was burning vigorously when my brother walked across the yard holding the limp but still living kitten in his palm.

"He's hurt," he'd said. "He's dying. This is the kindest thing to do." And he dropped the mewling kitten into the fire.

All I could do was stare at him. I could not speak, could not breathe or accuse him. The kitten was hurt because he'd hurt it. He'd skewered that helpless eight-week-old baby creature on a coat hanger then burned it alive and called it kindness. I was sickened, outraged, horrified. But did nothing.

Did you just hear me?

I did nothing. Said nothing. Told our father nothing when he asked about the missing kitten. When my older brother lied boldfaced to him for the God-knows-how-many-eth time, I averted my face. And said nothing.

Nothing.

Of all the regrets of my life, it is not the sins of commission that dominate. I've done what I've done, and mostly I've learned something and moved on. A step-cousin of mine once took seven years to decide on a color to paint her living room. That's nuts, you know? It's just paint. Stop thinking and thinking and re-thinking is what I wanted to tell her. Stop analyzing every damn thing to death.

Try shutting off all the little voices, especially the crippling perfectionist within, and start feeling instead. It's just paint. Go with your gut reaction, with the chip that makes you smile. Or laugh. Or relax. Or get your blood up. Paint the whole damn room whatever color makes you feel the way you want to feel in that room, in that house. And then, when it doesn't make you feel that way anymore, repaint it. It's just paint.

I've made many, many, many mistakes. Thank God. At least I made them. I. Made. Them. Actively. The worst mistake you can make is to be so afraid of making mistakes that you do nothing at all.

I waited most of my life for that mythical life-changing fork in the road that all the well-intentioned advice implied would present itself. What a crock. While I was preparing for that one big decision, I barely noticed the hundreds of thousands, maybe millions, I made without dreaming how significant they were.

That day my brother tortured and killed a kitten was one of them. I wish, I wish, I wish I could relive that one sin of omission. But the groundwork was already laid for me to put up, shut up, and take it on the chin. I realize that now. Our family motto was: Admit nothing; confess never; put nothing in writing. We were to keep our family business to ourselves. Answer no questions. Cover each other's backs. Keep our eyes and ears open and our mouths shut.

So I never told. Anyone. Ever. Until now. Honestly, I can't say I feel any better for it. And I don't see what it has to do with my case, but I may not get another chance. So there it is.

We lived in the trailer a couple of years, most of my time in junior high. I had a couple of close friends and spent as much time at their houses as possible. Anywhere but home.

Then along came Alice. Fat Alice, as we called her behind her back, At Falice. But not at first. At first, I was thrilled. My prayers were being answered.

I don't even remember being aware that my dad was dating. So when he sat us down to tell us he was getting married, I was confused. Married? When? Where? How? Who was she? When was in two weeks. Where was in our church. How was with our pastor. Who was someone he'd met back when we lived in Muskegon. Alice, he said. And I thought immediately about Alice in Wonderland and Alice Through The Looking Glass, and was ready to be charmed, to be mothered. Eager to have another adult around to keep an eye on us.

My older brother was openly hostile toward her from the beginning. My younger brother spent much time giggling at the thought of our dad having sex. I opened my heart. Stupidly.

Of course, another adult meant the trailer was too small and certainly not good enough for a woman of her caliber whose father was, after all, a doctor and so had been raised to expect much better.

So, six weeks before the end of my ninth year of

school, we moved again. Into town. Into a little white story-and-a-half with an apple tree in the back yard. Those last six weeks in a new school system with yet another curriculum passed in a fog. Moving in and out (then in and out again) of "new math" which I realize now was simply pre-algebra, had taken a toll on my attitude toward formal education as a whole. Educational philosophies and methodologies and schedules and rules and regulations fluctuated from school to school, so I again found solace in the one thing that did not change: English. I read as if my immortal soul depended on it. Voraciously, indiscriminately, incessantly, insatiably. Reading also shielded me somewhat from the disintegration of my home life.

It didn't take long. As I think I said earlier, Alice and my dad were married only a year and a half, but it seemed like a decade.

The house on Barnard Street was a number 6 house, supposedly all about the kids. And in a perverse way, it was. But not in any warm fuzzy toys and games and framed school pictures way, although God knows there were games. Oh yes. Games aplenty.

Alice was childless with no clue how to deal with kids in general, and I'm sure we would not have been easy to handle in any case. Our family dynamic was set. She was determined to dismantle and restructure it to fit her vision of an ideal family. We were determined not to let her. I could tell you a couple dozen specific episodes of our conflicts, of her attempts to control us, to control our dad, to drive wedges between us at every opportunity. But really, it's probably all stereotypical of step-parents everywhere. We thought she was insane, cruelly and unusually insane. A true nutjob.

Their marriage was pretty much over by the time I tried to kill myself, but I didn't realize it at the time. And actually, I didn't really want to die. I just wanted the pain to stop. I just wanted out. When the razor blade turned out to be too dull to slice through the skin at my wrists, I ate an entire bottle of aspirin. Don't laugh. Now I know that aspirin won't kill you, but then I didn't. As you can imagine, I got very, very sick.

Having a mother was definitely not all it was cracked up to be. Three examples should give you a general idea. One day she gave me a black eye for not wearing what she'd laid out for me. Another day, she screamed to my younger brother that he was not our father's son but a bastard by our whoring mother. And then she took the refrigerator. She piled all the food on the counter and took the refrigerator.

She could have taken the counter tops and the sink and the toilet and the light bulbs right out of their sockets for all we cared. She was gone.

Only one good thing came of our entanglement with Alice: my older brother graduated from high school and joined the Army. He was out of the house and out of my nightmares.

Through it all, I read.

Recently, I read about a man who has total recall of over 9,000 books. I have only the vaguest recall of a handful, but might well have read thousands. At one point, I toyed with keeping index cards of the books I read. I even formatted the entries: Title, Author, Plot, Main Characters, and Most Memorable Quote. But I didn't keep it up long. Somehow, documenting my reading list seemed to demean the books themselves. To me, they were not merely black marks on white paper between covers. They were friends. They accepted me just as I was, were open to me at any time of the day or night, asked nothing of me in return, so how could I organize them, analyze them, judge them?

Of course, now I wish I had.

Being the new kid in school so often taught me several things, not the least of which is that the kids most likely to accept the new kid are the "bad 'uns" as my grandmother would have said. So my friends were usually those on the fringes, as I suppose I was, too. They were the rule-breakers, hell-raisers, laughers, jokers, drinkers, smokers. So I tried all of the above. Drugs weren't part of the rebellion palette yet, although later I would try them, too. But somehow, through it all I could not manage to get rid of my virginity until I was 16, though God knows I tried.

We stayed in the house on Barnard Street all my time in high school and beyond. Although I made human ones, too, books were still my best friends. Each semester I would take home all my text books— geography, history, civics and all—and read them through by the end of the first week. If you think this behavior led to me becoming an A student, you are sadly mistaken. For once the books were read, I was ready to move on, but there was still a whole semester left. I spent much of my class time staring out windows or reading smuggled-in literature. I endeared myself to damn few teachers, as you can imagine.

What a hellacious job teaching must be. Day after day of trying to impart knowledge to hundreds of kids whose job is to resist learning. How many students, do you think, are truly engaged in that process? One in a hundred? One in a thousand? Give me drywall any day. Think about it: At the end of the day, at the end of the week, you can stand back and see the evidence of your efforts. You can run your hand across it to see what needs a bit more compound, a bit more sanding. You can prime it and paint it and Voila! A finished product. Your vision, your efforts, made manifest.

Or barbering. I've often thought I should have gone to barber college. When Ashley was a tot, I bought a book on how to cut your own or anyone else's hair and can't even guess how much money I saved over the years by cutting the kids' hair by myself. Sure, it grows back, but again, you have something to show for your efforts. And imagine, after a day's work of barbering, a dozen or so people look better and feel better about themselves. It's practically a humanitarian profession.

Sorry. I got sidetracked there. None of this is relevant, I'm sure. I'm getting to the end, I guess, and am afraid of leaving out an important detail. All that's left, really, is to explain my sexual self. The side of me that got me into this mess in the first place. Sex and men, men and sex. The deadly combination.

While we were living in the house on Barnard, I got a job at a drive-through ice cream parlor. I was only 15, so my dad had to sign my working papers.

If I told you how much I got paid an hour, you'd laugh. But remember, it was a long time ago. Why the boss left two teenagers alone to run the shop is beyond me.

But he did. I'd been babysitting since I was 12, using the money to buy fabric so I could make my own clothes. I never much liked what was on the rack, and then there was my own rack to deal with. If a dress fit me everywhere else, it pulled tightly across my breasts, squashing me or, if there were buttons in front, leaving gaps for leering male eyes. So I learned to sew so I could craft clothing that fit me better and that better expressed my personality which I seldom allowed others to see any other way.

I'd fended off my share of disgusting old father-types who volunteered to drive me home after a babysitting session, and I'd brushed off the ogling of my dad's cronies, and I'd spent years evading the unwanted attention of my own brother. In other words, I'd lost my face. I don't mean in the Asian term for shame or embarrassment or esteem; I mean that from the age of 12 or so, I noticed that people in general, but most specifically men, never looked me in the eye. They talked to the fat globules stuffed into my bras.

Now, don't get me wrong. It isn't that I was a prude, afraid of or ashamed of the idea of sex. Quite the opposite. My hormones were raging as furiously as any 15 year-old's. And remember: I was a reader. I read a lot about sex, too, and about love. So I could easily have used any handy male for sex; there seemed to be an abundance of them. But my fantasies of the deed itself involved someone I truly cared about who truly cared about me.

Don't laugh. I still believed it was possible. There would be long, soulful kisses and slow, loving caresses and deep, explosive passion after which we would hold each other closely, breathing deeply in the afterglow. I know, I know, I read too much. But there it was. Curious and eager or not, I was not about to squander my virginity on any of these crass oafs. I wanted a crass oaf of my very own.

But I was curious and eager, eager to shed this oppressive mantle of virginity and had taken a few tentative steps toward that goal. But the furthest extent to that time was to allow an attractive but pale young stranger to fondle those selfsame breasts in a dark movie theater. I never saw him again and didn't want to. As shameful as the act might have been, the feeling was delicious. The skin of his hand against the skin of my breasts, exploring, fondling, tweaking. I liked it. Very much. But I didn't want more. Not from him. Does that sound odd? That I allowed a stranger to do what so many others had tried? The difference, you must see, is that I chose him. And that it was all so gloriously anonymous. No one from my school would ever know about it. Although many claimed intimate knowledge of my body, they all lied. All their boasts (which invariably found their way to me) were embarrassing and infuriating, but not completely humiliating because they were not true.

I had never so much as held hands with anyone from

my own school, and I intended to keep it that way.

So I tolerated the ludicrous behavior of the boys in the halls and in my classes. I ignored them when they whispered or whistled or made those disgusting slurping noises as I walked by.

And it was the same at work, only worse. Because people drove through for their double-dip on a sugar cone or whatever, and because we took the orders on the driver's side of the car, and they were more likely to be men driving, their line of vision aligned perfectly with my bust. That was nice for them; they didn't have to strain their vision by looking down the whole time they talked to me. They could just conveniently fasten their gaze on my shirtfront. In school, I could clutch my books in front of me, wear the baggy sweaters, and pretend I didn't hear the remarks about "Shorty with the forty." But at this job, I was subjected to the most offensive leers and comments and lip-smacking and laughter. And true to my passive acceptance of abuse, I just took it all without comment.

But inside, I was seething. Revolted and repulsed. Furious at the piggish behavior of men in general. That is just what they seemed to me: greedy, slobbering piglets scrabbling for the mama's teat. What was so fascinating about breasts anyway?

I was a hell of a lot more than walking tits, but no one seemed to notice. Until Hank.

He drove in one late afternoon in his funky old flat black '52 Chevy. I don't remember what he ordered, but I was instantly taken by his eyes. A pale bluish gray, his eyes were leveled at my own. His lopsided grin, his self-deprecating shrug, his ease in responding to my suddenly light-hearted banter all charmed me in that first brief meeting. It was as if he were looking at me. Not my body, not the external me, but me. My person. He came back the next day, and the next, and the next. It took him a week to ask my name, but each time I saw him I could see he was looking at me. Into me. Deeply into my eyes. After a month, he asked me out.

But I couldn't go. My dad had a strict rule that I had to be 16 to date. And I knew my dad. Six weeks before my birthday might as well have been six years. We had to wait. Sort of. We found the loophole: driving me home from work so I didn't have to walk in the dark wasn't technically dating. Neither was sitting in our driveway talking for hours in that funny old car.

God, I wish I could remember what we talked about. But I don't. All I remember is smiling a lot, laughing a lot, and feeling his magnetic pull. Sitting on the front porch, hip to hip on the porch step wasn't dating either. So we'd kissed before our first date.

My dad thought Hank was goofy. But then, my dad didn't like many of my friends. Once he asked me if I attracted the kooks or the kooks attracted me. I had no response to that, not even a smart-assed one, like, "birds of a feather flock together." At the time I was defensive of my friends and offended by the question. Today, I must admit I've known some pretty odd ducks and loved them dearly.

On the night of my sixteenth birthday, Hank and I had our first real date. We went to a drive-in movie and watched very little of it. I was sure I'd found my soul mate and was fully prepared to seduce him into seducing me. Don't laugh, but at the time we called it necking and petting. I have no idea what the kids of today call it, but it amounted to everything but the deed itself. The deed itself was called "it," as in, "Did you guys do it?" And I was ready for the deed itself, ready for "it," or "going all the way," but Hank—well, let's just say Hank was very good with his hands. In the two years that we dated—on and off—I think I managed to get him to cross the line maybe three times.

One problem was that he was determined to be a good Catholic boy, and I was equally determined to be a very bad Lutheran girl. So we were equally matched, in a way. He was also afraid to get me pregnant. Maybe the deeper problem was that I truly wanted him and he truly loved me. At least, that's what I have chosen to believe all these years. It is preferable to the alternative that no one has ever truly loved me, for me. I've been wanted, and I've been needed. I've been useful—at least for a while. But Hank is the only one who ever made me feel truly loved. He loved me enough not to want to fuck up my life. So of course I had to do that for myself.

Maybe you've wondered how someone of reasonable looks and cleanliness could manage to remain celibate in these days of sex-saturated images, references, and innuendoes. In case you're thinking of trying it, let me assure you that it is relatively easy. First, you need the motivation. Since The Business With Tim, not only have I been terrified to allow myself to get too close to anyone for fear of what deep and ugly secrets I may let slip in an unguarded moment, but I have also been only too painfully aware of the messes I got into by letting the wrong part of my anatomy make my decisions. I've been such a fool for desire. Just imply by a too-lengthy glance that you could want me, and I'm all spread legs and open heart. An easy mark for the latter-day vampires who masquerade as lovers.

The eyes may be the windows of the soul, but they are the open doors to the bedroom. So I learned simply not to look. I could never trust myself to judge potential lovers wisely, so I learned the secret of avoiding the preliminaries: no eye contact. A glance never established cannot be maintained. And, as far as the urge goes, believe it or not, it goes away. Sort of like muscle tone: If you don't use it, you lose it. And the longer you go without it, the less you need or want it. True, for a while I was on some weird kind of bi-monthly cycle, the peak of which would find me just about tearing out my hair with the shrieking desire to be desired, the aching need to be wanted. But this, too, would pass, especially when I'd focus on enumerating the poor choices I've made in bed partners and the price I've had to pay for these poor choices.

If you are hoping for some vicarious thrill garnered by a gratuitous recounting of my sexual history, I'm afraid you are about to be sadly disappointed. I have no intention of exposing every episode. In the first place, it has nothing to do with the problem at hand. In the second place, despite your reassurances, I have no guarantee that this confession will not someday fall into the hands of my children, by which time they will have learned the worst anyway. But I will say that mere names, numbers, and places won't tell you about my philosophy toward sexual engagement. That is, if the love of wisdom is not a contradiction when applied to sex.

You see, even when I was still a virgin, I did not view sex as something I would let someone do to me, but as something I would do with someone. I never saw myself as a passive receptacle at all. I wanted what I wanted and I knew how to get it. Once, I read that women give sex to get love; men give love to get sex. But I gave sex to get sex. It just seemed most honest to approach the act as a mutually exchangeable commodity. For me, there was no particular confusion between love and sex. I did not expect to fall in love with the object of my desire of the moment, nor did I expect any of them to fall in love with me, although both of those things occasionally happened. I viewed my sexuality as just that: my sexuality. Key word: My. Mine. As in belonging to me. As in I decide.

And so it was that I repeatedly broke Hank's heart. My need would be too great to sublimate. Someone would catch my eye, and I would break up with Hank so I could go be that wild child. Then I would go back to my strong-willed and altogether honorable Hank, who would inevitably take me back. And we would be warm and loving toward each other (but only to a point, of course). Then it would start all over again. For all these years, I've thought it odd that Hank never threw my bad behavior in my face, never seemed jealous or resentful.

Only just now had it occurred to me that, rather than being long-suffering and saintly, maybe he simply didn't know what I was up to on our breaks from each other. I never told him, and he never asked.

Saginaw was both a small town and not all that small. I just assumed he knew; assumed someone would have told him. I also assumed the day would come when he would not take me back, that one day I would go too far.

As a matter of fact, I have assumed too much for too long. Probably stupidly. What a comfort assumption can be, and what a trap. It is certainly too late now to find the courage to ask. To assume nothing.

Finally came the day we were visiting one of his buddies who lived in an upstairs apartment on North Bond. Situated just a few houses from the corner, the apartment had a clear view of busy westbound one-way Davenport Street. The obnoxious sound of some asshole's too-loud car drew me to the windows.

"Who the hell is that?" I asked as the red Corvette cruised by.

"Oh, that's Christiansen," said Hank, moving behind me to glance out the same window with his chin resting on top of my head.

"Scott Christiansen. He went to school with us. No girl can get him."

"Bet I could," I said.

And I did, as I've already told you. Maybe I meant only to see if I really could. Maybe I thought I'd end up back with Hank. Maybe I wasn't thinking at all. Within four months, I was pregnant with Amber; within two more months, Scott and I were standing in front of the Justice of the Peace, making promises neither of us intended to keep.

And so we come full circle. The house tour completed. The sun sinking quickly. The end of the road. The end of my rope. All the final clichés.

Such a freaking waste of a life. No point in regret and everything to be sorry for. But if I could afford the luxury of regret, I'd start with religion.

If Hank slipped up, all he had to do was go to confession. He'd say he was sorry and have to recite some prayers of contrition as many times as the priest would require. Then he'd be forgiven. Just like that. I would love to have a religion that gives me the opportunity to confess. And then to be forgiven. To have to perform some act that would clean my slate. What a wonderful idea. How clean and simple. I have longed to confess, to share the burden of what I've done. But I can't.

Hell's bells.

THE END

With Amber safely back home to her husband, I'd had time to think, not that I'd done much else during the remainder of her visit. More than once, I know, I irritated her with my preoccupation and inattention which she quite naturally took personally. But what could I do? Tell her? Confess to my own daughter? Unburden myself by burdening her? I could do that no more than I could control my thoughts, my fears. And my macabre fantasies.

What would Tim look like now? How long would it be before they tracked me down? Before they ruined my children's lives? And how could I stop it? What could I do? What should I do? How far would I be willing to go? From the relatively benign to the thoroughly malicious, the various scenarios whirled through my mind. One by one I've tried them on like the perfect fit in shoes.

Sweet reasonableness might work. I imagined the

dialogue: "Excuse me," I'd say. "Do you remember me? My daughter and I stopped by last week. Remember? We used to live—"

"Live here. Sure I do. Can I get you a brewski?"

In this fantasy, Sam still had a can of beer in his hand. Maybe I'd judged him too harshly. Maybe it was a prop, like Bob Dole's ubiquitous pen, meant to detract from a handicap, but calling attention to it instead.

Sure.

Could be.

"I remember you saying you intended to tear out the front steps to build a wraparound deck."

"That's right. Startin' next week."

"Well, I was thinking about that." (Only I'd drop the final g as he did. What was that called? Oh yes, mirroring.) "Sounds like a lot of extra work. Why don't you simply build the deck over the top of the steps? Then you could have the deck just a half step down when you step out the door. Easy access."

"Well, now, I hadn't thought about that. But now you mention it, that's a damn fine idea. Save me a lot of work."

"Yes, yes it would. And it would preserve—" (No, not "preserve." Save. Yeah. Save.) "—my babies' handprints. I know they don't mean anything to you, but to me—" (Maybe I could even fake a tear or two here. Maybe I wouldn't have to fake them; maybe they'd come on their own.) "Maybe I could even help you build it? I've done quite a bit of building projects. No decks, but I could learn. You could teach me in exchange for my help."

And I'd be just that careful not to say "assistance" or "apprenticeship" or any other word over two syllables. Then, maybe: "I'll take that beer now, if you're still offerin'?" Dropping my g's.

And then, of course, I'd have to follow through to make sure he never broke that cap, never emptied that porch.

Oh sure. That wouldn't be suspicious as hell. Why not just walk up with a big old Guilty As Sin tattoo across my forehead? But the helping thing might work.

What if I went back there and offered to help if he'd teach me to build a deck, but be a little flirtatious? Amber'd said he seemed interested. Not that I was flattered. I've lived too long and seen too much to be flattered by the attentions of a bleary-eyed alkie. Or any man, maybe. I no longer believed that it took much to attract a man.

All those magazine articles and all those books on how to get a man to notice you are such a waste of pulp. Maybe I'm just jaded, but it seems to me that most men have very few requirements. A pulse, basically, and a certain willingness. And if he's an alkie, he'll settle for the willingness. It's all in the eyes. All in the eye contact. Look a man in the eye and he'll assume you are interested. So, I'd look him in the eye—what had he said his name was? Oh yes, Sam. And I'd let him think what he wanted to. Then, after a couple of beers (but I would need to monitor my own consumption very carefully, as I have such a low tolerance for alcohol) and a few too-heartily appreciative laughs at his undoubtedly lame attempts at humor, I might pretend to get a sudden brainstorm and then suggest building over the porch instead of tearing it out.

But what if he expected me to sleep with him? Move in with him? Marry him? I am certainly ready to do whatever it takes to keep that flipping porch intact and would be willing to pay any price. But I really don't want a romantic encounter with poor old Sam.

Maybe I could simply offer to buy the house back. It might take everything I've managed to squirrel away, but wouldn't it be worth it? Another trait of the cynical: believing that everything is for sale, everything has a price, everything is negotiable. What if I simply asked him to sell the house back to me? I could claim sentimental attachment, regret at ever having left. I could pay cash. Give him 30 days. Hell, 60 if he needed it.

I could.

But I didn't want to. I didn't want to move back there. And, depending on his asking price, I might have to sell my current house, too. So renting out the Lincoln Road house wasn't an option. Or was it? Renters wouldn't be tearing out porches. Most renters are not willing to put any of their own money or sweat into a house that isn't theirs. But if something went wrong with the furnace or the water heater or the well, they'd be calling me to come fix it. So I'd still have to go back inside that cursed house. Unless I hired the work done. But damn I hate spending money I don't need to spend.

Maybe I could just kill Sam. Maybe the second time is easier.

Too bad the house was cinder block. Fire wouldn't

harm it enough. An explosion would work, but I don't know much about explosives. Granted, the internet could help, but I have no way of knowing how much time is left to educate myself. Gas? Maybe gain access to his gas stove, extinguish the pilot light, then turn on the jet. Not all, you understand, just one. Leave a frying pan on the stove with some eggs nearby. Like he was overcome when he was going to fix himself something to eat. A grilled cheese sandwich, maybe. But I don't know if he has a gas stove. I'd had electric when we lived there. I've always been afraid of gas. Had there been a gas hook-up? I can't remember.

Poison? I know some things about poison, mostly from reading possibly hundreds of murder mysteries. Not chemicals, you understand, not rat poison or antifreeze, nothing obvious or that would be suspicious. Nothing that could be traced. All-organic poisons, nice healthy ways to kill someone or make them very, very sick. And very, very sick is sufficient if they already have compromised health. The leaves of tomato plants or rhubarb, potato sprouts that in a salad would look very much like bean sprouts. Mushrooms that look a lot like morels unless you really know your morels. Apple seeds, but it would take a whole cup full. And how would I get them down him? Spoiled seafood or meat? I've read some really nasty ways of killing people. But spoiled meat smells so bad, must taste so bad. How to get it down him?

Could I make it look like suicide? Men are more likely to commit suicide in noisy, messy ways—guns, mostly. I don't think I have the stomach for that. Blood and guts and gore. Remember, Tim's death was relatively neat and clean. Not much to clean up but urine. Not that I'd have to clean up after Sam. I'd be long gone. But I'd have to see it. Nope. I can't even watch gory movies.

Hanging wouldn't be bloody. But how on earth could I manage that? I've built up some muscles over the years, but since I finished my current house, I haven't had much heavy hauling and lifting to do, so I've lost most of my upper body strength and haven't time to buff up now. And I pretty much doubt I could ask him to pretty please come stand under this beam in the garage while I place this clever hangman's noose around his adorable neck. Even drunk, Sam would probably not be complicit in his own lynching.

Alcohol is an excellent method of suicide but so damn slow. He'll poison himself eventually, but by then—?

Maybe he is on medications of some kind, something that might not be a good idea to overdose on. But again, that would require me to infiltrate his life, his house, that damnable house. I do not want to set foot inside that house again. Not if I can help it.

So if I can't go back, I have to go forward. Hell, maybe I can disappear. I've thought of this many times throughout the years. How easy it would be, I've thought. Purely out of curiosity, I even sent for a booklet on how to create a new identity. For $29.95 plus mailing, I got a poorly-written, poorly-constructed booklet that had obviously been printed, folded, and stapled at someone's kitchen table. So I wasn't sure how credible the information was. Still, I kept it. I put it in a file folder marked "water bills" and stuffed it in the bottom drawer of my household filing cabinet. I put other things in there, too, things I have no legal right to possess.

I've already told you the worst of the things I've done. Why should I be reticent to tell you about this, too?

I know it is wrong, a federal offense in fact, to keep misdirected mail. I know the right thing to do is to return it to the mail stream. I know this. But, as you know by now, I am not always able to do the right thing. Sometimes I do the most expedient thing, the easiest thing. Sometimes I do the most interesting, the most intriguing thing. So when a new mail carrier on my route delivered an envelope addressed to a woman who had lived in my house years ago, I opened it. I could tell you I opened it by mistake, not really looking at the name on the front until I examined the inside. But that would be a lie. I've tried to be honest with you and see no reason to stop now. I can't even tell you why I opened that envelope; it was just an impulse. The glue hadn't stuck all the way across the flap, so I slid my thumb under it and opened the envelope without harming it in the least. I intended to snoop a little, re-seal the envelope, and drop it in the mail collection box at the post office. Inside was a retirement statement from the state. She either works or did work for the State of Michigan. Her retirement benefits didn't interest me, but another line of numbers did: her social security number.

According to that piece-of-shit booklet I'd gotten suckered into buying, a valid social security number was key in establishing a new identity. The letter also (and stupidly, irresponsibly if you ask me) gave me her birth date. If I took her identity, I could make a new life somewhere else, somewhere far away from a poorly-constructed concrete porch that was already crumbling from too much sand in the bloody mix. As an added benefit, I could also shave nine years off my life.

Inexplicably, I did not return the misdirected envelope to the mail stream. I saved it in that same "water bills" folder. And then I added another. About a year ago, a substitute UPS driver, not my usual nice guy, tripped (she said) on the uneven approach to my driveway. In all honesty, there is a crack there, but anyone can clearly see it, so I thought her claim was bullshit. She scraped her precious little knee and went to the emergency room, for crying out loud, the damn baby. When her insurance wouldn't pay for what it considered non-emergency treatment, and UPS workman's comp wouldn't pick up either, she sent me a copy of the bill from the hospital and a poorly-spelled letter demanding that I pay it out of pocket and clumsily alluding to a possible small claims suit.

In my response to her, I suggested that the next time she sent someone a copy of such a document, she might want to block out her social security number, which was clearly printed at the top of the form, along with, of course, her birth date. I very thoughtfully and considerately warned her that this sensitive information, in less scrupulous hands, could be used to steal her identity, to cause havoc in her personal and financial life.

Needless to say, she dropped her claim. This document, too, I carefully filed. One never knows, I thought, but I had no specific plan. At least not at the time. With her identity, I could shave a full 12 years off my age. With a new identity, I could put the Lincoln Road business with Tim behind me forever.

This fantasy strikes me as the most preferable, so I've spent the most time entertaining it. As long as I (or my identity donors) keep out of serious trouble, I reason, I can live indefinitely free of the possibility of capture. I've already learned to avoid relationships that might tempt me to disclose anything incriminating. I've even become comfortable in a solitary, secluded life. With enough cash—it will have to be cash, at least at first—I can go anywhere. I can go to Canada; there are plenty of places to get lost in Canada. I can go to Australia; I've always dreamed of going to Australia and have read many novels set there. I can go to Mexico or South America, even. The only option not open to me is to stay in Michigan. Michigan has become too small for me now. In Michigan, I would never be free of the possibility of running into someone who knows me, who might speak to me, who might call me by my true name.

Selling my house will be the first step. From past experience, I know that a house sometimes sells faster when it is overpriced. At least twice in the past this tactic has worked for me. When a rehab didn't sell quickly enough to suit me, I'd up the price, much to the consternation of the real estate agent, and—presto! It would sell. My theory is that a certain breed of people tends to look in price ranges; a lower-price house is strangely not as attractive as a higher-priced one. Maybe they enjoy doing that long-suffering reverse-bragging thing. You know what I mean: they sigh and complain that they paid way too much for something so they can let people know they have the money to pay too much. I'll sell everything I can't pack into my truck, give the kids the few family pieces I own, make up some story about seeing the U.S.A. in my Chevrolet and shove off.

As advised by the booklet I bought, I'll apply first for a copy of Amy's birth certificate. Then, with my new identity secured, I can secure a replacement social security card. Then a driver's license. But not in this town, just in case anyone at the DMV went to school or worked with or is related to the new me. Then a passport. But how long will all this take? Weeks? Months? Do I have months? Weeks? Days? Hours?

And can I really leave my kids? Can I bear never to see any of them again or hear any of their voices? Even if it is for their own good? For their own security? I've sacrificed so much already.

I might have loved again, maybe even married. I might have gone to college. I've always dreamed of getting a degree, but in what? For what? I've loved books all my life, but what good is a degree in literature? I've always been drawn to masonry, too. Almost went to school for that. Almost went to barber college. Almost. Almost.

But every time I almost did any of the things I wanted to do, I thought of Tim. I thought of the secret I held deep in my conscience. And I was afraid. Loose lips sink shits, and I have been one shitty shit. No amount of dog or cat rescue or anonymous donations to worthy causes or random acts of generosity or prayers for the healing or blessing of others can atone for what I did to Tim. If I relaxed for one second, if I trusted even one person, if I dared to let my guard down the slightest sliver, it could all be over. For my kids and for me.

Sometimes I've thought it would be easier if Tim had planted me instead of the other way around. At least I would not have had to live the half-life I have. Sometimes, in the darkest crevices of the darkest moments of the darkest days, I have wished I had died instead of Tim. Just think: the dead have no regrets. We living face them hourly.

I most sincerely regret every mean, selfish, impulsive, hateful thing I have ever done. I regret every mistake I've ever made, from what I did to Tim to slapping Amber's face when she was twelve and told me she hated me. But most of all, I regret every chance I did not take, every opportunity I was afraid to accept, every risk I've ever run from. I've played it safe, and for this I am unutterably sorry. And believe me, I'd take my own life if I could.

But I can't. Again, I'm too much of a coward. I don't want to bleed or to hurt. I don't want anyone to have to clean up after me, wash my brains from the wall. And I don't want my kids to have to deal with a maternal suicide any more than I want them to deal with a maternal murderer.

Unless I could make it look like an accident. Like I'd slid out of control on icy streets, but black ice is months away, and—again—I don't know how much time I have left. Is Sam fondling his sledgehammer as we speak? Imagination is so damn unreliable.

Shit. Shit. Shit. Shit. Shit. Shit. Shit.

Any way I cut it, I need first to find out how much time I have.

I must go back to Lincoln Road. I must go home again.

NOTE FROM "AMBER": INSERT B

I listened to the tapes and had nothing else to do, so I transcribed them. I have no freaking clue what my mom was doing with all this garbage. And I do mean garbage.

First of all, I have no idea why she lied about all this. Well, not all, but most. Some. Hell, I don't even know. She does have three kids. Did. No, does. And we did take a drive past all the houses I'd lived in. Others, too. Ones she'd lived in, but who cares how far she had to walk to school or how bad the apples smelled in the fall when they fell in the back yard or what color she painted her bedroom and how hard it was to find a paint store that would tint it as dark as she wanted.

And she told the truth, surprisingly, about how often she just checks out on us, just follows her thoughts wherever they lead. Irritating as hell is what that is. How hard could it be to just focus, for God's sake?

But the killing people crap? My mom wouldn't hurt a fly. A mosquito, maybe, but I swear to God, I've seen her open a door so she can let a fly or bee or ladybug escape unharmed. Spiders, too. She'll catch a spider with a slip of paper, an envelope or whatever's handy. Coax it onto the paper and take it outside.

So, kill someone? Hardly.

And "Tim"? That wasn't his name, of course, although as I typed up her ramblings, I caught one place where she used his real name. I corrected it like I did some of her verbal quirks and grammatical mis-steps. Cleaned it up for her.

After all, I wasn't in a big yank to go back home. I've made my own matrimonial mistake. When I go home, I'll have my own mess to clean up, my own tough decisions to make. Or to implement. The decision is already made.

I couldn't find him on the Internet, not even the Social Security Death Index. "Tim," I mean. He did sort of disappear one day when we kids were staying with our grandparents, and all his stuff was gone. We never saw him again but didn't care. We were relieved, actually. What a jerk.

And the porch was suddenly finished after being dragged out over the summer, but—

Well, it's just not possible. What she said. No way. Not my mom.

So I've hung around her place a couple more days, trying to figure out where on God's green earth she is and veering between confused, irritated, and deeply concerned. Where the hell is my mom?

ABOUT THE AUTHOR

Molleen Zwiker was born in Panama and raised in Michigan. In the first grade, she wrote and illustrated her first short story on a length of coarse brown paper towel purloined from a roll in the girls' restroom. Her grandmother saved that story, and Zwiker still has it, filed with everything she's ever written. Almost everything. When she was 24, she began her first novel, a scathing feminist view of an inverted future where men are second-class citizens. Startled by the bitterness she read in her own work, Zwiker torched that manuscript. This she sorely regrets; there was a market for bitter, after all. Zwiker earned an MFA in Creative Writing, Playwriting, from Western Michigan University. Currently, she is working on a new novel tentatively titled *The Art of Murder.*

ACKNOWLEDGMENTS

Every successful creative project is by nature a collaboration. Many hands, hearts, and minds contributed to this book. Friends read and commented; acquaintances read and critiqued. Family encouraged and supported. Some held my hand and some kicked my butt. My gratitude goes to all of them.

Thanks also to the staff and contributors of Scribe Publishing Company, who have also been godsends, including:

Jun Ares, for designing an amazing cover to bring my book to life. He is a talented designer who can be reached at aresjun@gmail.com.

Paul Ennis, for his sharp eye, unerring instinct, and excellent editing skills, and…

Jennifer Baum, for including *Unreliable* in Scribe Publishing Company's first collection.

CPSIA information can be obtained at www.ICGtesting.com
Printed in the USA
BVOW072344200613

323899BV00002B/4/P